Alison Roberts is a New Zealander, currently lucky enough to be living in the South of France. She is also lucky enough to write for the Mills & Boon Medical Romance line. A primary school teacher in a former life, she is now a qualified paramedic. She loves to travel and dance, drink champagne, and spend time with her daughter and her friends.

AWAKENING THE SHY NURSE

ALISON ROBERTS

MILLS & BOON

First published in Great Britain 2020
by Mills & Boon, an imprint of HarperCollins*Publishers*
1 London Bridge Street, London, SE1 9GF

Large Print edition 2020

© 2020 Alison Roberts

ISBN: 978-0-263-08586-0

MIX
Paper from
responsible sources
FSC™ C007454

This book is produced from independently certified FSC™ paper to ensure responsible forest management. For more information visit www.harpercollins.co.uk/green.

Printed and bound in Great Britain
by CPI Group (UK) Ltd, Croydon, CR0 4YY

PROLOGUE

'WHAT'S THAT?'

'Nothing.' Annalise Phillips tried to fold the sheet of paper and stuff it back in the envelope at the same time. Her nonchalance didn't quite work and her younger sister Abby narrowed her eyes suspiciously.

'That's envelope's got a window. It's a bill, isn't it?'

'It's nothing to worry about. I've got everything under control.' Lisa watched as Abby manoeuvred her wheelchair to the other side of the kitchen table. She'd always been able to convince Abby that she could manage and that had turned out to be an accurate prediction for so many years that it had become an automatic and genuine reassurance. So why was Lisa aware of a nasty edge of panic approaching this time?

'Look…' It was good that there was a distraction on hand. 'There's a letter here for you as well. No window.'

'Really?' Abby transferred her laptop from her knees to the table and reached for the letter. 'Oh…maybe it's confirmation of my date to sit my driver's licence.' She grinned at Lisa. 'I still can't believe you managed to find that funding for my modified car. It's the most exciting thing ever…'

It felt good to be able to smile and tap into the glow of having achieved something that had been such a long time coming. Abby didn't need to know that Lisa hadn't exactly found funding from a charitable community support organisation and she had, instead, taken out a huge loan against the house to pay for the modifications the car had needed to accommodate a paraplegic driver. Or that the first repayment of the loan was now due at such an unfortunate time when she was between jobs, having been forced to resign from her nursing home position due to a merger that would have meant she had to move to another city.

'Oh...*oh*, you're not going to believe this...' Abby sounded as though her new car had just been demoted from being the most exciting ever. She handed her letter to Lisa. 'There's a room available at the uni hostel. Ground floor, with an en suite bathroom—one of the ones that are only available to disabled students. And get this... it's an unexpected vacancy because a student has pulled out of her course so I can move in next week!'

'Next *week*?' Lisa took the sheet of paper but she couldn't focus on the words. 'But... but...' She had to swallow hard. She wasn't ready for this after all.

Abby was waiting for her to look up. 'You knew this was coming, Lise,' she reminded her gently. 'I've had my name down for one of those rooms in that hostel ever since I started uni and that's years ago.'

'I know.' Lisa tried to find that smile that seemed a million miles away now. 'And it's wonderful. You're going to be completely independent and I'm so proud of you and... and...would you like a cup of tea?' Lisa got to her feet quickly to escape her sister's watchful gaze. 'Wait, no...we should be having a drink to celebrate, shouldn't we? Have we got any wine?'

'We never got round to opening that fizz when you found out about your new job. You said that seeing as you weren't starting for more than a month, we might as well keep it on ice, but maybe now is the perfect time.'

'Mmm... I think it is.' Lisa busied herself finding the bottle in the back of the fridge, getting glasses down from the high cupboard and then opening the sparkling wine. It certainly seemed like a good idea. Abby wouldn't know that she might be drowning her sorrows instead of celebrating, would she? Or panicking because she needed to find enough money to pay a rather large bill in the very near future?

But, of course, her sister knew her better than that. How could she not, when Lisa had been pretty much her principal carer for as long as she could remember? Her only family since their grandmother had died nearly ten years ago now.

'What's really up, Lise?' she asked quietly.

What could Lisa say? That she was beginning to wonder if she'd made a big mistake applying for that desk job as a junior manager in another nursing home just because it had regular hours and was close to home and would make life a lot simpler? That living alone in this little house they had inherited from Gran suddenly seemed like the loneliest prospect ever and it would give her far too much time to worry about how Abby was coping. Worse, it would be more time to revisit the guilt that it was her fault in the first place that her sister was having to cope with so many more challenges in life?

No. She couldn't go there. They'd agreed long ago that it was so far in the past it was a no-go subject. That you could destroy your future if you didn't leave your past behind...

But she couldn't be dishonest either. 'I'm going to miss you,' she told Abby.

'I'll only be on the other side of town. I'll drive you crazy with how often I visit.'

'And I'm only a phone call away.' Lisa

nodded, taking another sip of her wine. 'If…
you know…'

'If I fall out of my chair, you mean?' Abby
laughed. 'I can manage. It's a long time since
I've needed you hovering around like a helicopter parent.'

It was meant as a joke but Abby must have
realised it stung a bit because she reached
out to touch Lisa's arm. 'It's not that I don't
appreciate everything you've done, you
know that, don't you?'

Lisa nodded. And took a longer sip of her
wine.

'You've been—and still are—the best sister ever but it's time we both got to live our
own lives. It's the next step for me and then
I'll really be able to have a place of my own.
Where I can bring my boyfriend home. Or
you can bring yours, at least.'

Lisa's jaw dropped. 'You've got a boyfriend?'

'No, silly.' There was a beat of something
very dark in the way Abby avoided her gaze.
Avoided allowing a memory any hint of the
light of day in the hope that it would stay

buried for ever. It was another reason that Lisa felt the need to stay close to Abby to be able to protect her. If she hadn't come home when she had that night, they both knew what would have happened because Abby had been unable to defend herself.

'You'd be the first to know if I did.' Abby's tone was too bright. 'I've been way too busy getting my Master's in occupational therapy to want the hassle of a man in my life again. And now I'm well into my postgraduate course in hand therapy so I'm still too busy but, for heaven's sake, Lise—you're nearly thirty and you haven't had a proper boyfriend yet and it feels like that's at least partly because you think you have to keep looking after me.'

'I have had boyfriends,' Lisa protested. If Abby was determined to deal with her past trauma by burying it, then all she could do was support her. She made her own tone light and bright as well. 'I've had lots of them. There was Michael. And Stephen. And…um…what was his name? Oh, yeah… Geoffrey. I guess he doesn't really count…'

Abby was laughing again. 'None of them count. They were all the most boring men on earth. Stephen wore socks and sandals and the most interesting thing he had to talk about was his worm farm. Michael was so skinny and tall and bald he looked like one of the test tubes in his laboratory and…oh, my God… I'd forgotten about Geoffrey. Wasn't he the one whose mother turned up on your first date?'

The wine was definitely helping because Lisa was laughing now, too. 'I think he'd booked a table for three all along.'

They'd seemed like such nice men, though. Safe…

'You're right,' she had to admit. 'I have a talent for picking boring men.'

'Being bored is bad,' Abby declared. 'I think that's your problem at the moment. You haven't got enough to do until you start your next job. You should go on a holiday.'

Lisa's breath escaped in a huff of laughter. As if. She'd never been on holiday in her life and she certainly wasn't about to start now. Not when money was so tight it was scaring her.

'What I *should* do is find a job for a few weeks.'

She didn't realise that she had voiced the thought aloud until she saw the frown on Abby's forehead.

'Why? Oh…it's because of my car, isn't it? I *knew* it cost too much…'

'No.' Lisa shook her head. 'It's because I need something to do so I don't die of boredom. I'll go crazy rattling around here by myself for weeks after you move into the hostel. I might end up on your doorstep every day.'

'Can't have that.' Abby feigned horror. 'Fill up those glasses again.' She opened her laptop and started tapping keys. 'I'm going to see what's on offer for a super-talented nurse who only wants a few weeks of work. Hmm…we need a high-end medical locum agency, don't we?'

By the time Lisa had their glasses brimming again, Abby was looking triumphant.

'I've found the *perfect* thing. Tailor-made.

It's work but it's a holiday at the same time. And it's legit. This agency—London Locums—is obviously highly rated.'

'What is it?'

'A cruise. More specifically, a Mediterranean cruise. Oh…' Abby's sigh was heartfelt. 'It starts in Spain and then goes to places in the south of France and Italy and some Greek islands before finishing up back in Spain again. How romantic is that…?'

The countries and islands were fantasy destinations. A cruise ship even more of a fantasy but not one that Lisa had ever considered desirable.

'I couldn't do that. Cruise ships are full of self-indulgent people who have too much money and just want to float around having a good time, eating and drinking far too much. It would be disgusting.'

It certainly went against the values Lisa Phillips had embraced since she'd been no more than a child.

'There's nothing wrong with having a good time occasionally.' Abby was watching her sister again. 'It might be fun. They need a nurse in this ship's well-equipped infirmary, just for a two-week cruise, to fill in a gap in a team of two doctors and three nurses. You'll get time off to go on shore at some ports of call and accommodation and all meals are provided. And they'll pay top rates for the right person. Why don't you give this woman a call tomorrow? Julia, her name is...'

Lisa's attention had certainly been caught. Not so much by the idea of shore excursions in foreign parts or shipboard accommodation or even the novelty of working in a completely different kind of environment. There was, however, something that made this feel like it might be meant to be—probably the words "top rates".

'Show me...' She leaned closer as Abby turned her computer so she could see the screen. 'Oh, wow...they're paying *that* much? And it doesn't start until after next week so I'd be here to help you move.'

Lisa pulled in a deep breath. 'I think you're right. It *is* perfect...'

CHAPTER ONE

WEARING JEANS HAD been a bad idea.

It was much hotter than Lisa had expected in Barcelona and, by the time she climbed out of the taxi after her trip from the airport to the port, it felt like the denim was actually sticking to the back of her legs. Even her short-sleeved white shirt felt too warm, despite her having removed her light cardigan. She could only hope that the uniform Julia from London Locums had told her would be supplied for her temporary job as a ship's nurse was better suited to a late summer Mediterranean climate.

The friendly taxi driver opened the boot of the car to retrieve her small, bright red suitcase. 'Here you go, *señorita*.'

'Thank you so much.' Lisa dug in her bag to find her wallet. 'I don't suppose you know which of the ships here belongs to the Aqua-marine cruise line?'

Her driver shrugged. 'It's no problem. See that big round building over there?'

Lisa looked over her shoulder and nodded.

'That's the World Trade Centre. Your ship will be one of the ones berthed around it.'

Lisa could see the massive ships docked around the building. They looked like float-ing cities and one of them was going to be her home for the next couple of weeks. Maybe those butterflies in her stomach weren't solely due to the nervousness that came from starting any new job. Maybe they were due to something she didn't have that much experience of...like excitement? She could feel a smile tugging at the cor-ners of her mouth as she turned back to pay her driver but for a split second her gaze snagged on what was happening over *his* shoulder.

Another taxi had pulled up. The rear door was open and a man had stepped out. A tall, lean, *ridiculously* good-looking man... He was wearing light, casual clothing and looked as though he'd just spent a very re-laxing day of sightseeing and highlighting those streaks of sun-kissed blond in his hair. To add to the impression of sheer pleasure, she saw the long, long legs of his compan-ion emerging from the back seat of the car. Slim, elegant arms went straight around the man's neck as the woman got to her feet and he leaned in to kiss her with a leisurely grace that suggested it was by no means a first kiss and more like a continuation of a sexy, afternoon romp.

'Um… Here you are. Is that enough for a tip?' Embarrassed, Lisa was fumbling with the notes and coins. The embarrassment wasn't just because she didn't know about tipping practices in Spain. It was more to do with what was going on just a few feet away from her. That *kiss*… It was still going on. And on. For heaven's sake, it was broad daylight. Those two needed to get a room. Again…?

'Enjoy your time before you set sail,' her driver instructed. 'You can walk to Las Ramblas from here in less than fifteen minutes. If you have time, take a tour on the bus. This is the most beautiful city in the world.'

Lisa nodded her thanks for the advice but she knew she wouldn't be exploring Barcelona today. Arrangements for her urgent passport hadn't been finalised in time for her to join the cruise along with all the new passengers in Malaga a couple of days ago so it felt like she was playing catch-up already. She was due on board her new place of employment at four p.m. and that was… she glanced at her watch…less than twenty minutes from now, which didn't give her that much time to identify the correct ship to board. Being late was the height of rudeness as far as Lisa Phillips was concerned.

As her taxi pulled away she noticed that *that* kiss was finally over and the leggy blonde was—reluctantly—getting back into her taxi. As Lisa pulled the long handle out of her suitcase the man lifted his hand in a farewell wave and then turned, his gaze locking onto Lisa's a heartbeat later. He had to know that she'd seen what he'd just been doing but he didn't seem remotely bothered. If anything, that quirk of his eyebrow seemed like nothing more than a flirtatious invitation. Perhaps *she* might like to find out how good at kissing he was?

Lisa could feel colour flooding her cheeks as she snapped the handle of her suitcase into place and then tipped it so she could start dragging it behind her. She'd already had a sneaking suspicion that it wasn't just the sightseeing and unlimited food and drink people took cruises for and that had just been confirmed. Some people clearly found a cruise an opportunity for unlimited sexual adventures as well. A "what happens on board stays on board" kind of thing.

'Can I be of some assistance?'

Oh…dear Lord… The man's voice was just as gorgeous as the rest of him. Deep and sexy and with a hint of laughter that went with his whole, laidback look. It had to be the overly warm air she was dragging into her lungs that was adding to the heat Lisa could feel in her cheeks. And in the pit of her stomach, come to that. A rebellious corner of her brain was melting in that heat as well. Otherwise, why would it come up with the absurd idea that maybe she *would* rather like to find out how good this man was at kissing?

'No,' she said firmly, without looking up, so he wouldn't notice her fiery cheeks. 'Thank you, but I'm fine. It's not heavy and I'm perfectly capable of managing by myself.'

'No problem.' That hint of laughter was more pronounced now. 'Enjoy your cruise.'

A group of women, in flowing maxi dresses and floppy sunhats were coming towards them. Amidst the giggles, a call came that sounded more like a command.

'Hugh… You must see these photos we took at the beach today. Wait until you see Scout's new bikini.'

He'd already slowed his pace so it took only seconds for Lisa to leave him behind with the young women. Fellow passengers from the same ship, she decided. Hopefully not hers. She quickened her own pace, heading towards the first ship that was towering over her more and more as she got closer.

There was a covered gangway sloping up to a door on the side of the hull and a desk shaded by a canopy at the bottom, staffed by uniformed people who might well be able to help her. If this wasn't her ship, they could no doubt point her in the right direction.

Well, well, well… So there were still women in the world who blushed?

Hugh Patterson was intrigued, he had to admit, as he strolled along the marina, having finally extricated himself from the group of overexcited young women that he really didn't have the energy for after a long lunch with his Spanish friend, Carlotta. Well acquainted with the tourist circuit of the Mediterranean for a couple of years now, Hugh had friends in many of the popular cruise ship destinations.

It wasn't just sailors that had a girl in every port these days, he mused. Ships' doctors could be just as privileged and if you were that way inclined, it was the easiest sex life ever because anybody involved knew that it was never going to be anything serious.

It was just intermittent fun. Living life for the moment and enjoying every minute of it.

That young woman he'd made blush at the taxi rank had looked as if she needed to learn to let herself enjoy the moment. Fancy being so uptight you wouldn't even let someone help with your suitcase? Or even make eye contact with them when they offered? Maybe it was actually irritating rather than intriguing? Being dismissed like that was not something he was used to.

'Hi, Hugh. Had a good day?'

One of the team welcoming people back on board the ship after their shore excursions saw him heading for the gangway.

'Fabulous, thanks, Simon. I love Barcelona. I had a picnic with a friend in Parc Guell.'

'Oh…lucky you, not having to work today. I don't get a day off on shore until Santorini this time. Or it might be Mykonos. One of the Greek islands, anyway.'

'I know… I'm lucky. We only need one doctor on board at all times when we're in port so, with two of us, we can take turns.'

He did feel lucky. What other doctors got to do their work in what could seem like an endless holiday but still got to practise enough real medicine that it didn't get boring and it was also possible to keep one's skills honed? Okay, he'd probably want to settle down sometime in the future but not yet. Maybe never, in fact. He'd almost done that once and look what a disaster that had turned out to be.

'I'm about to go and take over from Peter now, though,' he added, heading towards the gangway. 'That way he can at least get out and stretch his legs on land.'

Hugh took the stairs rather than the elevator to get to the lobby atrium of the ship, which was one of the most impressive areas on board with its marble floors, glittering chandeliers, huge potted palm trees, and the grand piano that was always providing some background music for the crowds taking advantage of the boutique shops and bars that circled the lobby on several levels.

Except old Harry wasn't playing his usual repertoire of popular classics. He wasn't playing anything at all but standing beside his piano stool, looking down at a knot of people at the base of one of several staircases that curved gracefully between the atrium levels.

What was going on? Hugh's pace increased as he got close enough to see that someone was on the floor in the middle of the group. An elderly woman, who, despite what had to be well over thirty-degree heat today, was wearing quite thick stockings. One of her shoes had come off and was lying beside someone that was crouched at the woman's head.

'Let me through, please,' he said calmly. 'I'm a doctor. What's happened here?'

The crouching person looked up and Hugh was momentarily startled to see that it was the blushing girl from the taxi rank. Right now, however, she was supporting an elderly woman's head in a manner that suggested she knew what she was doing to protect and assess a potential cervical spine injury.

'She fell,' he was told. 'From about halfway down these stairs. Her neck seems to be okay, though.'

'Did you see it happen?'

'Yes... I was almost beside her going up the stairs.'

'Please...' the victim of the fall raised her hands. 'Just help me up. I'm fine... I really don't want to cause such a fuss.'

'We need to make sure you're okay first,' Hugh told her. 'My name's Hugh and I'm a doctor and this is...' He raised his eyebrows at the young woman who had, he couldn't help noticing, rather extraordinary eyes—a golden hazel shade but the edge of the iris had a dark rim around it, as if nature had been determined to accentuate the design.

'Lisa,' she supplied. 'My name's Lisa and I'm a nurse.'

No wonder she was giving the impression of competence, Hugh thought, as he focused on his patient. 'What's your name, love?' he asked.

'Mabel...'

'Is anything hurting, Mabel?'

'I... I'm not sure... I don't think so, dear.'

'Can you take a deep breath? Does that hurt?'

'No...'

'Is someone with you?'

'Frank...my husband...he's coming shoon. We need to shee about our...our...'

Hugh frowned. Mabel might look to be well into her eighties but that didn't mean she might not have been having a drink or two this afternoon. But slurred speech could very well be an indication of something more serious as well—like hypoglycaemia from a diabetic emergency or a head injury, which was not unlikely given the hard marble flooring beneath her.

'Was she knocked out?' he asked Lisa.

She shook her head. 'I don't think so but, if she was, it would have only been for a moment because I was beside her by the time she got to the bottom of the stairs. I tried to catch her but I was just a split second too slow, unfortunately.'

This Lisa might be small but Hugh could imagine her leaping into action to try and

help someone. She was still clearly determined to help.

'She didn't just fall,' Lisa added. 'She
looked dizzy. She was already holding the
railing but she let go and...' Lisa was watching the elderly woman carefully. 'Mabel? Do
you remember that?'

'No...pleashe...let me up...'

Hugh was holding Mabel's wrist, finding
her pulse rapid but very pronounced, so her
blood pressure couldn't be low enough to
explain any dizziness.

'Move back, folks.' Old Harry, the pianist,
had come down from the stage and was trying to move people further away. 'Let's give
them some space.' He caught Hugh's gaze.
'I'll go to the infirmary, shall I? And get
some help?'

Hugh nodded. 'Yes, thank you.'

Mabel pulled away from his hand and
moved as if she was making an effort to sit
up.

'Don't move, Mabel,' Lisa said. 'Let us
look after you for a minute, okay?'

But Mabel tried to roll and then cried out with pain.

'What's hurting?' Hugh asked.

'Look…' Lisa tilted her head to indicate what she had noticed. 'That looks like some rotation and shortening of her left leg, don't you think? A NOF?'

Fracturing a neck of femur was a definite possibility given the mechanism of injury and they were often not that painful until the patient tried to move, but Hugh was impressed that Lisa had picked up on it with no more than a glance.

'Try and keep still, Mabel.' Lisa leaned down so that Mabel could hear her reassurance. 'It's okay…we're going to take care of you…'

The warmth and confidence in her voice was as distinctive as her eye colouring. She sounded absolutely genuine—as if she was well used to taking care of people and doing it extremely well. If Hugh were unwell or injured, he would certainly feel better hearing that voice. Mabel was trying to respond but seemed to be having trouble getting any words out and that was when Hugh noticed the droop that was now obvious on one side of her face. Lisa's observations that it had appeared to be a medical event that had caused the fall rather than a simple trip and the other symptoms like the slurred speech now were coming together to make it urgent to get this patient into hospital.

It was a relief to see the other ship's doctor, his colleague Peter, coming into the lobby, with the emergency kit in his arms. One of their nurses was following and she carried a pillow and a blanket under one arm and an oxygen cylinder under the other. Hugh had another flash of relief that they were currently docked in the port of a major city. They might be very well equipped to deal with emergencies on board but someone who was potentially having a stroke and had fractured their hip in a fall would have needed evacuation to a land hospital as quickly as possible. At least they wouldn't need to call in a helicopter this time.

'We need an ambulance,' he told Peter.

'Not just for the NOF. We've got signs that the fall might be the result of a CVA.'

'We'll get them on the way.' the older doctor nodded.

'Mabs?' An elderly man was pushing his way through the concerned spectators. 'Oh, no...what's happened?'

He crouched down beside Lisa, who moved to let him get closer to his wife. Hugh turned to reach into the emergency kit as Peter opened it. They needed to get some oxygen on for their patient, check her blood glucose level, get an IV line in and some pain medication on board and to splint her hip. They needed to talk to Mabel's husband, too, and find out about her past medical history and what kind of medications she might be taking. It was only when he looked back to start talking to Frank that he realised that Lisa had disappeared. Did she think she might be in the way now that the rest of the ship's medical staff were on scene?

It was a shame she'd gone, anyway. He would have liked to have thanked her. And to tell her how helpful she had been.

* * *

Lisa should probably have introduced herself to the ship's doctor and the nurse who'd come in with him and she should have offered to keep helping, but after she'd moved to let Mabel's husband get close enough to comfort his wife, the nurse had moved in front of her and it just hadn't been the right time to say anything that might interrupt the focus on their patient so Lisa had let herself slip into the background to let them do their work. She would have expected that good-looking passenger who also happened to be a doctor to stand back and let the people in uniform take over but it almost looked as if he was still in charge of the scene.

Moving further back brought Lisa to the bottom of the staircase and she took a few steps and then paused to watch what was happening. She might be doing this herself very soon, dressed in pale green scrubs with a stethoscope hanging round her neck like the nurse who was currently taking Mabel's blood pressure. The doctor, in a crisp, white uniform with epaulettes on the shoulders of his shirt, was attaching electrodes to monitor Mabel's heart and the extra doctor... Hugh... was sorting something from what looked like a well-stocked kit. IV supplies, perhaps?

She could only see Hugh's profile but she'd been much closer to him only a minute or two ago and she'd been aware from the instant he'd appeared that this was a very different man from the one who might have been flirting with her near the taxi rank earlier.

It wasn't that he was any less good looking, of course. Or even that that relaxed grace that came from an easy enjoyment of his life had vanished. It was more that there was a focus that made it obvious this man was intelligent and he knew what he was doing. Lisa could respect that. She could forgive him for being some kind of playboy, in fact. After all, doctors were just like any other professional people and there were no laws that prevented them going on holiday and letting their hair down occasionally, were there?

Onlookers were being asked to leave the

area and make space as a team of paramedics arrived with a stretcher. Lisa found herself in a flow of people that took her to the next level of the atrium but she knew she needed to find an elevator or internal stairway. Not that there was any point in finding the ship's medical centre to introduce herself when she knew the staff were busy here for the moment, but her suitcase would have been delivered to her cabin by now so it would be a good time to find out where that was and freshen up before she went to meet her new colleagues.

She did know she had to go down rather than up. Crew members didn't get cabins with balconies. They were possibly right in the middle of the ship and might not even have any portholes. Lisa had to hope that she wasn't prone to seasickness. Either that, or that the Mediterranean was a very calm sea.

An hour or so later, Lisa was heading for the middle of Deck Two, where a helpful steward had told her the medical centre and infirmary were located. She had showered, swapped her jeans for a more formal skirt and brushed her short waves of auburn hair into a semblance of order. A large red cross painted on a steel door told her that she had found her destination and a sign below that gave the hours the medical facility was open and phone numbers for the nurse on duty for out of hours. So, it was a nurse rather than a doctor that made the first response to any calls?

Lisa's heart skipped a beat as she went into an empty waiting room. She was going to be one of those nurses for the next two weeks, with possibly more responsibility than she'd ever had before if she was going to be the first responder to something major like a cardiac arrest or severe trauma. This time she knew that that internal flutter was definitely excitement. She was stepping well out of her comfort zone here, and…well…she couldn't wait…

'Hello?'

The desk at one side of the waiting room was empty. Lisa peered around a corner and walked a short distance down the corridor.

There were consulting rooms, a room labelled as a laboratory where she could see benches covered with equipment that looked like specialised blood or specimen testing machines and a closed door that had a sign saying it was the pharmacy. An open door on the other side of the corridor showed Lisa what looked like a small operating theatre. Surprised, she stepped into it. There was a theatre light above the narrow bed in the centre of the room, a portable X-ray machine, cardiac monitor and ventilator nearby and glass-fronted cupboards lining the walls that looked to be stocked with a huge amount of medical supplies.

A movement in her peripheral vision as she entered the narrow corridor again made Lisa turn, to see the back view of the white pants and shirt of the ship's doctor's uniform as he stood at the desk in the waiting room.

'Hello...' she said again, walking towards him. 'I was starting to wonder if I was all alone here.'

The doctor turned and Lisa could actually feel her jaw dropping. If she'd thought this man was good looking when she'd seen him kissing his girlfriend, it was nothing to how attractive he looked in uniform. Especially *this* uniform, with the snowy, white fabric accentuating his tanned skin and making those brown eyes look remarkably like melted chocolate. He also looked as startled as Lisa was feeling. They both spoke at precisely the same time.

'What are *you* doing here?' Lisa's voice was embarrassingly squeaky.

'It's *you*...' His tone was more than welcoming. It was almost delighted.

They both stopped speaking then and simply stared at each other. Lisa was confused. Why was Hugh wearing the same uniform as the ship's doctor? And, now that they were nowhere near someone who needed medical attention, why was it that the first thought that came into her head as she looked at him was the image of him kissing that woman so very thoroughly? To her dismay she could feel heat creeping into her cheeks.

It was Hugh who finally broke the awkward moment, his mouth curving into a lazy smile. 'You're blushing.' He sounded amused. 'Again...'

Oh, help... So, avoiding eye contact with him out on the pier hadn't been enough to disguise her beetroot-coloured cheeks, then. Lisa closed her eyes as she sighed. 'I'm a redhead. It kind of goes with the territory.' She opened her eyes again, frowning. 'I thought you were a passenger.'

'But you knew I was a doctor. We've just been working together.'

'Yes, but... I thought you were a doctor who was on holiday.' Good grief...the look she was getting suggested that it was Hugh who was confused now. He probably thought that she was an idiot. 'I'm Lisa,' she added. 'Lisa Phillips. I'm a—'

'Nurse,' Hugh put in helpfully. 'Yes, I remember. A good one, too, I think. Thank you for your help earlier. With Mabel.'

'It was a pleasure.' The compliment about her abilities was making her feel far more proud of herself than it merited. 'Do you know how she is?'

'I believe she's doing well. She's scheduled for hip surgery later this evening but the better news was that her neurological symptoms had virtually resolved by the time she reached the hospital.'

'So it was a TIA rather than a stroke?' A transient ischaemic attack could present with the same symptoms of a stroke but they were temporary. A warning signal rather than a critical event.

'So it would seem.' The quirk of Hugh's eyebrow told her that he was impressed by her medical assessment but then his smile reappeared. 'Now…what it is that I can help *you* with, Lisa Phillips? I hope you're not unwell…or injured…'

Along with a very genuine concern in his voice, there was a gleam in those brown eyes that made Lisa remember that kiss all over again. Or rather the moment he'd caught her gaze after the kiss and they'd both acknowledged what she'd seen. There was also an acknowledgement of something on a different level—one of mutual attraction, perhaps? Oh…help… Lisa looked away. Any attempt to return the man's smile evaporated instantly. She'd never expected to see him again and things were about to get even more unsettling.

'I'm a nurse,' she explained.

'Yes, I know. A nurse on holiday.'

'No... I'm here to work. Through London Locums. I believe I'm replacing someone called Amanda who needed time to support her mother who's having surgery?'

There was another moment of startled silence. 'You're our *locum*? Why didn't you say something?'

'Why would I? I thought you were a passenger.'

'But you didn't say anything when Peter turned up.'

'Peter?'

'Our other doctor. And Janet was there— one of our nurses.'

'Well...it didn't seem quite the right moment to be introducing myself.'

'I guess not. Let's do that properly now, shall we?' Hugh was holding out his hand. 'I'm Hugh Patterson. Pleased to meet you, Lisa. I look forward to working with you for the next couple of weeks. And it will be me you're working with mostly because you're filling a gap on my Blue Watch.'

'Oh?'

Lisa had taken his hand automatically but, instead of shaking hers, he simply held it for a moment and then gave it a slow squeeze, and that did it. Like a switch being flicked on, an electrical jolt shot from Lisa's hand and raced up her arm—an extraordinary tingle she had never felt before in her life. It was enough to make her pull her hand free with the kind of instinctive reflex she might have had to touching something that was hot enough to burn her badly.

How weird was that?

And this Hugh Patterson was looking forward to working with her?

'Yes,' he said, as if confirming her silent query. 'I'm Blue Watch. Peter's Green Watch. It just means that we'll be working together. Probably having the same days off as well and you should be able to get some shore excursions if there's space. Do you have a favourite place to visit around the Mediterranean?'

'This is the first time I've been out of England,' Lisa confessed.

'Really?' Hugh sounded astonished. 'You don't like travelling?'

'I've…um…never really had the opportunity, that's all.' Lisa wasn't about to tell him the reasons why. He didn't need to know about her family responsibilities and he certainly wouldn't be interested in hearing about financial hardship. This Hugh Patterson looked like one of life's golden people who never had to worry about anything much. Someone from a completely different planet from her own, which made her wonder how well they might be able to work together. Perhaps he was thinking along the same lines now because the look she was receiving made her feel as if she was being seen as someone very unusual. Someone… interesting?

The prospect of her new working responsibilities pushing the limits of her professional comfort zones were nothing in comparison to how this man was pushing the boundaries of anything she considered personally safe when it came to men.

No wonder she'd snatched her hand back as if she was about to get burned.

Anyone who had anything to do with Hugh Patterson could be playing with fire. Lisa could feel herself releasing her deeper than usual breath carefully. It was nothing to worry about because she never played with anything dangerous. Never had. Never would. That there was even any temptation there was enough of a warning that she wasn't about to ignore.

'I'm looking forward to working here as well,' she heard herself saying with commendable calmness. 'And, if you've got a moment, I'd appreciate a bit of a tour, if you've got time, that is. I'd like to get up to speed as soon as possible—preferably before my first shift tomorrow morning.'

Lisa was edging back a little as she spoke. Even though she had broken the skin contact between them well over a minute ago, she could still feel that odd tingle it had provoked. It was almost as if she could still feel the warmth of his skin, filling the air between them, and when he spoke both his words and his tone made both those impressions even more noticeable.

'No problem,' he said. Those dark eyes were watching her so closely Lisa had the horrible feeling that he knew about that tingle. That he knew that she thought he was dangerous.

'Come with me,' he added, with that lazy smile that was already beginning to feel familiar—the one that suggested he was finding this all rather amusing and he intended to enjoy the entertainment as much as possible. 'I'm all yours, Nurse Phillips.'

CHAPTER TWO

OH, DEAR...

It was going to be too tempting not to tease this new colleague a little. There was something about her that made her seem much younger than she probably was. First appearances were giving him an interesting impression of someone being well educated and intelligent but possibly naïve at the same time. Hugh had never had a little sister, but if he had, he was quite sure he'd feel like this in her company. He could appreciate the fact she was gorgeous without being remotely attracted, feel proud of her ability to do her job well and perhaps recognise that there were things he could teach her. That, in the interests of being a kind, big brotherly sort of person, he had a duty to teach her, even.

Like persuading her that life could be significantly more enjoyable if she relaxed a bit? She was so tense. So eager to give the impression that she could cope with anything she might be asked to do. It seemed that this Lisa not only liked to be able to manage on her own when it came to carrying a suitcase, she was determined to get all the information she needed to be able to achieve the ability to manage alone in her professional environment if that should prove necessary.

'So...do you follow a standard protocol for resuscitation in cardiac arrest?' Lisa was clearly familiar with the model of life pack for cardiac monitoring and defibrillation that was on top of their rapid-response/resuscitation trolley. 'Thirty to two compressions to ventilation rate until an advanced airway is secure? Immediate shock for documented VT or VF and then every two minutes?'

Hugh nodded. 'You've got a recent Advanced Care Life Support qualification, I assume? That's one of the standard requirements for working on board a ship.'

Lisa mirrored his nod. 'I've had experience with laryngeal mask airways and administration of adrenaline but I'm not yet qualified for antiarrhythmic drugs or intubation.'

Something in her tone made Hugh curious. Or maybe it was the use of that qualifying 'yet'.

'What made you decide to go into nursing and not become a doctor?' he asked her.

There was a flash of surprise in her eyes that made him wonder if she wasn't used to people asking her personal questions—or that she discouraged them because she preferred to guard her privacy.

The response was no more than a verbal shrug, however. 'Why do you ask?'

'I just get the impression you'd like to be doing more. Like intubating someone in a cardiac arrest?'

Lisa's glance slid away from his. 'I always wanted to work in a medical field,' she said. 'Nursing was the most practical option at the time.' She turned to touch another piece of equipment that was close. 'Does this take digital X-rays?'

'Mmm…' Hugh was still curious but he knew when someone wanted to avoid talking about something. Had Lisa become a nurse because she hadn't been able to afford the time or costs to go to medical school? 'It can be helpful to be able to transmit an image, either for a second opinion—which we can get via internet links to all sorts of international experts—or to get the right treatment available as soon as possible if we transfer someone to a land hospital, by chopper, for instance.'

'Do you go with them?'

'Sometimes they might need a doctor on board if they're critical. If someone local doesn't come with the evacuation crew we might send Tim, who's qualified as both a paramedic and a nurse and covers a lot of our night shifts currently. Or you might even go as a medical chaperone, depending on what else is going on.'

It was a true statement but Hugh was telling her that she might be involved because he wanted to see her reaction and, sure enough, there was a gleam of interest in those amazing eyes at the prospect of being choppered off the ship and back again. A glow of excitement even, and that gave him an odd little kick in his gut. So, she was up for a bit of adventure, this Lisa, even if she was uptight. This was good. It could make teasing her even more enjoyable.

'And do you ever do actual surgery in here? It looks more like an operating theatre than an assessment or treatment area.'

'It is, at times.' Hugh told her. 'We have to be able to deal with every situation you could imagine and sometimes we're out of range of emergency transport for some time. We've got anaesthetic and ventilation gear along with the digital X-ray and ultrasound and a full range of surgical instruments, though I haven't had to use too many of them yet.'

'But you've got a surgical background?'

'I've mostly specialised in emergency medicine and critical care but I've got both surgical and anaesthetic diplomas as well. How 'bout you?' Hugh led the way out of the room. 'What's your background?'

'My early experience was working in A and E,' Lisa said. 'Which I really loved. But my last job as head of a nursing home team gave me a lot of scope for first response and medical assessment and that was interesting, too. I'm…between jobs at the moment, which was why a locum position was ideal.' She had paused to look through the door of the laboratory. 'What range of tests can you do on board?'

It seemed like asking Lisa a question only made him want to ask more—like why she'd gone to work in a nursing home if she'd loved the emergency department so much? And, if she'd had so much experience already, why did she give off this impression of…well, it was almost innocence. Unworldliness, anyway, and that certainly wasn't something Hugh normally came across in the women he met these days. He was curious, he realised. A lot more curious than he usually was when he met someone new.

'Again, we have to be prepared for as many things as possible. We can test for cardiac enzymes if we suspect a heart attack, infections, arterial oxygen levels and blood glucose levels and a dozen or more other things. Janet's our expert and she can give you a rundown on how to do the tests but it's mostly automatic so it's easy. And, speaking of Janet, she's in our little two-bed infirmary at the moment because we admitted a woman with a severe migraine earlier today for monitoring so let's go there and I can introduce you.'

'That will be great, thank you.'

Hugh watched as Lisa took a last, slow glance back over her shoulder towards the areas he'd already shown her, as if she was mentally cataloguing and memorising everything she'd learned so far, and he was almost tempted to give her a quick quiz but then her gaze ended by catching his and there was a note of surprise there. Or maybe it was criticism because she had expected him to be moving by now and taking her to the next source of information about her new job.

She could turn out to be bossy, he decided, once she had settled in and was confident of her surroundings and responsibilities, but he took the hint and led her towards the hospital end of the medical centre.

"Bossy" was the wrong word, he decided moments later. "Feisty" was probably a more accurate prediction. His internal correction made him smile.

Hugh liked feisty. He liked it a lot.

If he was any more laidback, he'd be horizontal.

But Lisa knew that this relaxed impression of complete confidence with a streak of an impish desire to liven things up a little was just one side of the coin as far as Dr Hugh Patterson was concerned. She'd seen him morph into a completely focused professional dealing with an accident scene and she saw the coin start to flip again as they entered the ship's hospital at the other end of the medical centre. There were two small four-bed wards, one for passengers and one for crew, separated by a nursing station currently staffed by the team's senior nurse. Janet was older, with a friendly face and a Scottish accent but they had no time for

more than a brief introduction before Hugh
picked up the chart for their inpatient.

'She's responded well to the treatment,'
Janet told him. 'She's had a good sleep, her
headache's down to a two-out-of-ten pain
score and she hasn't vomited since her first
dose of anti-emetic.'

Lisa saw the frown line of concentration
that appeared between Hugh's eyes as he
rapidly scanned the information on the chart
of medications administered and observations taken. Then he walked towards one
of the only two beds in the room, the frown
line evaporating as his mouth curved in a
reassuring smile.

'Rita, isn't it? I'm Hugh Patterson, one of
the doctors on board. It was my colleague
Peter who saw you this morning, yes?'

The woman on the bed, who looked to be
in her early forties, was nodding. 'I feel ever
so much better,' she told Hugh. 'Those pills
have been wonderful.' She was staring at
Hugh. 'Have we met somewhere before?'

His smile was charming but fleeting. 'I
don't think I've had the pleasure but I'm

very glad you're feeling better. I suspect the main thing that's helped was to give you something for the nausea and vomiting and fix the dehydration that was making things worse. This wasn't your first migraine, was it?'

'No, but I haven't had one for ages. I know to stay away from triggers like chocolate and red wine.'

'Are they the only triggers that you know of? Flashing lights and loud noises can do it for some people. You haven't been out partying in the nightclubs on board till all hours, have you?' His tone was teasing.

'I should be so lucky.'

Rita was smiling now. And blinking more rapidly, Lisa noticed. Good grief...was she trying to flirt with her doctor? Batting her eyelashes even? If so, at least Hugh wasn't responding with anything more than a hint of his earlier smile.

'Might be an idea to keep avoiding anything like that for a day or two. I'm sure you don't want to be stuck in here and missing out on any more shore excursions.'

'No…my friends all went out for a horse riding trek today and I was so looking forward to doing that. Oh…' Rita's eyes widened. 'I remember now. I *do* know you. You're *that* Hugh Patterson…'

'Oh?' Hugh was looking wary now. 'Which one would that be?'

'Your mother was Diane Patterson, yes? The District Commissioner for the Windsor pony club and you used to have a three-day event on your family estate every year. I rode in it more than once—oh, ages ago now but I remember you used to be on the quad bike, doing errands like delivering coffee to the judges.'

Wow… His family had an estate in Windsor? Somehow that didn't surprise Lisa. That laidback, making the most of good things approach to life often went hand in hand with extreme wealth, didn't it?

'Mmm… Ancient history.'

His clipped tone made it very clear that he had no interest in pursuing this line of conversation and Lisa dropped her gaze instantly when his glance slid sideways so she could let him know she wasn't interested in hearing personal information like this. She could understand perfectly well why he might be embarrassed at having his family's financial situation made common knowledge and she could sympathise with that. She might be completely at the other end of the financial spectrum but she wouldn't want strangers knowing about hers either.

'We'll be setting sail in the next hour or so.' Hugh was scribbling something on Rita's chart. 'What we'll do is take your IV line out and give you some medications to take with you.' He was turning away from this patient. 'Don't hesitate to call if you're not continuing to improve, though. One of our wonderful staff members will be available at all times.'

His smile became suddenly a lot more genuine as his gaze shifted to catch Lisa's and, for the first time, it was impossible not to smile back. He was making her feel so welcome and as though he really did believe she would be a welcome addition to their team, even though he had only just met her. There could be relief making that welcome more pronounced because he could get away from a conversation he obviously didn't want to have but it didn't matter… Lisa was going to make sure that Hugh wasn't disappointed with his new staff member.

Janet was also very welcoming and, after she had taken out Rita's IV line, dispensed the medication Hugh had prescribed and discharged her, the older nurse took Lisa to find her uniform and then continue her exploration of the ship's medical facilities as she heard about what her duties would entail.

It was during this additional tour that Lisa became aware of a background hum of sound that was new and an odd sensation that something was changing in the air around her. Janet smiled at her expression.

'We're underway,' she told Lisa. 'I love that moment when we leave shore and head out into the freedom of the open sea. It's what keeps me coming back every season.'

Yes. Lisa could recognise that it was the distant hum and vibration of extremely powerful engines that she could both hear and feel, and the realisation hit her that this massive vessel and the thousands of passengers and crew on board were soon going to be far from land and reliant on what suddenly seemed like a very small medical team to deal with any medical or traumatic emergency that might happen.

They were also on the way to somewhere Lisa had never been in her life and the combination of potential adventure and challenge was...well...it was enormously exciting, that's what it was. The hum and sensation of movement was coalescing somewhere in the pit of her stomach in a tingle that was not unlike the one she had experienced earlier today, when Hugh Patterson had been holding her hand, but this was far more acceptable. Welcome, in fact, because it was almost completely a professional kind of excitement.

Whatever this exotic position threw at her for the next couple of weeks, she was going to do her absolute best. She always did, of course, but there was an incentive here that was a little different from anything she'd experienced before. She had to admit that part of that incentive was a little disturbing, however. While it was perfectly natural to want to do her job exceptionally well for the sake of anybody who was ill or injured on this ship, and she'd always had that determination wherever she'd worked, what was different this time was why it seemed almost more important to impress her new boss.

I found your ship online. Looks amazing!

It's totally unreal. There are bars and restaurants open all night, shows like you might see on Broadway, fitness clubs and dance classes—you name it, it's happening on board this ship.

I found a page with pictures of all the important people who had lots of stripes on their shoulders.

They're the officers.

Lisa was curled up on her bunk, typing rapidly in the message box on her laptop screen. Conversations with Abby were both more reliable and a lot less expensive this way than by phone.

The ship's doctors were there too.

They're considered to be officers as well. The nurses get privileges too. We can go anywhere we like on board and not just keep to the crew quarters for meals and things.

Who's the doctor with the beard?

That's Peter.

And who's the other one? The really *really* good-looking one?

Hugh. He's the one I mostly work with.

Oooh... Lucky you.

A string of emojis with hearts instead of eyes made Lisa shake her head before she tapped back.

You're just as bad as every other woman on board. We had four of them in the clinic yesterday, all trying to outdo each other to get his attention and…get this…two of them had come in to ask for the morning-after pill because things had got "out of hand" the night before at some party.

Wow…not the best line to take if you want to get somebody interested, I wouldn't have thought.

Lisa was smiling as she responded.
No. And anyway there are strict rules about the crew fraternising with the passengers.

What about the crew fraternising with the crew???

It was a winking face at the end of Abby's message this time.

Not going to happen.

Why not? Is he single?

I haven't asked him.

Why not?

I'm not interested.

Oh...yeah...right... Why not? Because he's too good-looking? Doesn't wear socks with sandals?

Lisa leaned back against her pillow and closed her eyes for a moment. She'd been busy enough settling into her new environment in the last couple of days so that she could concentrate purely on her work and find her way around this enormous ship. There was a lot of work to do during the often busy open surgeries at the medical centre, which ran for a couple of hours both morning and early evening, where she was responsible for triaging any patients that arrived and dealing with minor cases that didn't need to see a doctor, like small lacerations or medication needed for seasickness.

Between those hours, there seemed to be plenty of administration to take care of, new people to meet and calls to what had so far proved to be easily managed situations in cabins or public areas of the ship.

But now that Abby was teasing her, there was no getting away from the fact that she was not immune to Hugh Patterson's charms, however confident she was in being able to resist them. Not that she'd had to resist them, mind you. He was both charming, friendly and great to work with, but it was patently obvious that she was a curiosity to him and she knew why. She'd seen one of the type of women he was attracted to, for heaven's sake, and she couldn't be more different to the sophisticated, confident and sexy blonde that had accompanied him back to the port in Barcelona.

The woman that he'd been kissing with such…thoroughness…

Oh, no…there it was again. That tingle that she thought she had actually conquered over the last busy days. Distraction was needed.

Lisa opened her eyes and started tapping again.

How are things for you? Do you still like the hostel?

Love it. It's so much easier to be close to campus like this and the food's great. Miss you, though.

Miss you, too. Got a date for your driver's licence test yet?

Next week. And guess what?

What?

I'm going to try out for a wheelchair basketball team. I need some more exercise, what with all the great food in the canteens.
Hope that's not as dangerous as wheelchair rugby.

Lisa hit the "enter" button before she stopped to think that maybe Abby wouldn't appreciate the warning but it had always been difficult not to be over-protective of her little sister.

Sure enough, she could almost hear the sigh that came with Abby's response. And she obviously wasn't the only one who would prefer a distraction.

Stop being a mother hen. Tell me about where you are. Have you been on a shore excursion yet?

Not yet. My watch was on duty for the stops in both Corsica and Marseilles. Next stop is Nice, though—tomorrow—although we actually stop around the corner in Villefranche sur Mer because this ship is too big for the Nice port and we have to take small boats to get in to shore. We dock at dawn and then the ship doesn't sail until about ten o'clock at night and I'm just helping with the morning surgery hours so I've got most of the day and the evening to go sightseeing.

OMG…on the French Riviera? You're living the dream.

I know.

Lisa found an emoji with a huge grin.

I'll send photos but try not to get too jealous.

Don't send a photo unless it's you and that cute doctor alone in some romantic French café. Preferably drinking champagne.

LOL Lisa sent back.

Give it up, Abby. Not going to happen.

But, despite any firm intentions, it was what she was thinking about as she shut down her computer, climbed into bed a bit later and switched off her light. Champagne. Delicious food. An outdoor eatery, maybe shaded with grapevines. Someone playing a piano accordion nearby. And a companion who was only biding his time before taking the opportunity to kiss her senseless. Lisa could actually feel the tension of that anticipation. The curiosity. Desire...?

No. She pushed it away, rolling over to find a cool patch on her pillow. She'd certainly never found a kiss that lived up to that level of anticipation. It was the stuff of romance novels, not real life. It was just easier to toy with fantasy when she was temporarily "living the dream", as Abby had reminded her. Floating on the Mediterranean in a luxury cruise ship. Heading for land in a country that was famous for romance as much as anything else.

And there she was again…imagining being on the receiving side of a kiss like the one Hugh had been giving the gorgeous blonde. Not necessarily with Hugh, of course…just a kiss like that.

Oh…who was she kidding? It had to be Hugh, she realised as she was drifting into sleep. She'd never even seen anyone kissing like that in real life—she'd only read about it, or seen it on a movie screen. But this wasn't real life, exactly, was it? Lisa was already deeply into a very odd mix of real life and fantasy and the lines between the two were already a bit blurred. About to indulge herself by drifting further towards the fantasy side, it was a rude shock to hear the strident beeping of her pager. She snapped on her light and reached for the small device.

Code One, the pager read. Lido Deck.

Lisa was out of bed and hauling on her uniform in seconds. There was no time to even think about what her hair looked like. Her cabin was the closest to the medical centre. She had to go and grab the rapid response trolley and head for the deck that had the swimming pools. Hopefully, someone else from the team would join her quickly but, for the moment, she knew she was on her own.

Her heart skipped a beat and then sped up as she raced along the narrow corridor towards the medical centre. This was definitely real life and not any kind of fantasy and she was on the front line. Lisa had no idea if any of the other medical staff would also be responding to this call, even if Code One was the most urgent kind of summons. She might well be on her own until she found out whether the situation was really serious enough to warrant extra staff at this time of night.

It had to be well after midnight by the time Lisa had commandeered a service lift to get her to the Lido deck as quickly as possible. Heads turned as she raced past people wrapped up in blankets lying on deckchairs.

It was a movie night where a huge screen had been lowered on the other side of the largest swimming pool, the deckchairs lined up in rows to accommodate the audience. Red and white striped bags of popcorn got spilled as a crew member in a white hat jumped out of Lisa's way. She passed restaurants that were still open and she could smell the variety of food on offer—from burgers to Indian meals.

There were people everywhere, laughing and having fun, even dancing in the area that Lisa was heading for where there was another pool and two spas, which made it feel quite bizarre to find a knot of crew members and others around a figure that was slumped against the side of one of the spa pools, wearing only a bathing suit.

Lisa could hear that the young man was having trouble breathing as she crouched down beside him, feeling for his pulse on his wrist. It was rapid and very faint, which suggested his blood pressure could be low.

'I'm Lisa,' she told him. 'One of the ship's nurses. Can you tell me your name?'

He opened his mouth but all she could hear was the harsh sounds of him trying to move air through obstructed passages.

'His name's Alex,' someone told her. 'We got him out of the pool because he started coughing and couldn't stop.'

'Are you asthmatic, Alex?' Lisa was pulling open drawers on the resus trolley. She needed to get some oxygen on her patient and probably a nebuliser to try and help him breathe.

'He's allergic.'

Lisa looked up at the young woman in a red bikini. 'To what?'

'Strawberries. He told me when he didn't want to try my strawberry daiquiri.'

'He said he had an adrenaline pen in his pocket,' A crew member added. 'But we haven't found where he left his clothes yet.'

'Okay...' Lisa slipped an oxygen mask over Alex's face. 'I'm going to give you an injection right now,' she told him.

Her own heart rate was well up as she located the drug she needed, filled the syringe and administered the intramuscular injection. An anaphylactic reaction could be a very satisfying emergency to treat if it responded rapidly to adrenaline and the frightening swelling in the airways began to settle, but it could also be a situation that could just as rapidly spiral into something worse— potentially life-threatening.

Waiting the few minutes to see if a repeat dose was needed gave Lisa a chance to take some vital signs and check Alex more thoroughly, and that was when she noted the diffuse, red rash that was appearing all over his body.

'You didn't drink the daiquiri, did you, Alex?'

He shook his head. He was holding the oxygen mask against his face and his eyes, above the mask, were terrified. Even through the plastic of the mask, Lisa could see that his lips were swelling.

'I kissed him.' The girl in the red bikini burst into tears. 'This is my fault, isn't it? He's not going to die, is he? You have to *do* something...'

She did. Nebulised adrenaline was the next

step, along with a repeat dose of the drug by injection but, even if that started to make a difference, Lisa was going to need help and, as if she'd sent out a silent prayer, the figure that pushed through the group of spectators was the answer she would have wanted the most.

Hugh Patterson.

'Fill me in,' was all he said. 'I've got some crew bringing a stretcher.'

'Anaphylaxis to strawberries,' Lisa told him. 'Diffuse rash, hypotensive, tachycardic and respiratory obstruction with stridor—oxygen saturation currently eighty-eight percent. First dose of adrenaline was about three minutes ago but there's no improvement.'

'No worries.' His nod let Lisa know that he'd absorbed all the information and he knew how serious this was. His tone was still laidback enough not to alarm anyone else, however. 'Let's get another dose on board. And can you set up a nebuliser as well?'

Lisa drew up the medication as Hugh put

a hand on their patient's shoulder. 'We've got this, okay? But we're going to take you down to our medical centre where we've got all the bells and whistles. I'm just going to pop an IV into your arm while we wait for your transport.'

Lisa knew her way around the trolley drawers by now so she was able to hand Hugh everything he needed before he had to ask. A tourniquet to wrap around Alex's upper arm, an alcohol wipe to clean the skin, a cannula to slip into a vein and then the Luer plug and dressing to secure the access. Lisa prepped the bag of saline by puncturing the port with the spike of the giving set and then running fluid through the tubes to eliminate any air bubbles. Hugh was attaching the line to the Luer plug as the crew members arrived with the stretcher and then helped lift Alex onto it.

'Carry that bag, please, Lisa. And squeeze it. We need to get that fluid in fast.'

They moved swiftly through an increasingly subdued crowd of people on the Lido deck, into the lift and then down to the deck they needed. Lisa was relieved that they would soon be in their well-equipped treatment room. She was even more relieved that she had Hugh by her side. They had just been working seamlessly, side by side, to stabilise this patient and she was sure that they would have things under control in no time.

'On my count,' Hugh said to the crew. 'Lift on three. One, two...*three...*'

Alex was being placed smoothly onto the bed as Lisa reached up to flick on the overhead operating theatre light and she caught her breath in a gasp of dismay as it went on. Alex's head had flopped to one side and his chin had dropped enough to close his airway completely. He had clearly lost consciousness.

Hugh heard her gasp and his gaze locked on hers—only for a heartbeat but it was enough for a very clear message to be shared. Their patient's condition had just become a whole lot worse. They were in trouble and Hugh was counting on Lisa's assistance. She could also see the determination not to lose this battle in those dark eyes.

Lisa tilted her head instantly in a nod to let Hugh know she had received the message. That she would do whatever she could to help. That she shared his determination to succeed. And then she took a very deep breath.

CHAPTER THREE

IT WAS VERY likely that other members of the medical staff on board were already making their way to help with a Code One emergency but the non-medical crew members who'd helped transport their patient were dispatched to make sure that Peter knew what was going on. In the meantime, the situation was escalating so quickly that Hugh and Lisa were the only people available to deal with it and they would have to work fast to save this young man's life.

The bag of IV fluid that Lisa had been squeezing to administer it more quickly was empty so she reached for a new one. Fluid resuscitation was an essential part of dealing with anaphylactic shock. As was oxygenation. As she worked to set up the new bag of saline she could see how smoothly

Hugh was working to tilt Alex's head back to try and open his airway and then, using one hand, to shift his stethoscope over all lung fields to listen for air movement.

'He's still shifting some air but it's not enough.'

Lisa checked that the clip on Alex's finger was secure and looked at the screen of the monitor, below the overly rapid spikes of the ECG. 'Oxygen saturation is down to seventy five percent,' she told Hugh. The automatic blood pressure cuff was deflating at the same time. 'His BPs dropping again. Seventy-five over forty.'

'Come and take over here. We'll swap the nebuliser mask and use an Ambu bag and a hundred percent oxygen. I'll get another IV line in and start an adrenaline infusion. I'm not going to wait if things deteriorate any more, though. We'll go for a rapid sequence intubation.'

Lisa could feel the fierce concentration when Hugh took her place by Alex's head a minute or two later to try and insert a breathing tube through the swollen tissues in their patient's mouth and throat. A lot of doctors might have panicked when not only the first but the second attempt failed. Hugh only looked more focused. He caught Lisa's gaze as she moved back in with the bag mask and tried to deliver oxygen to Alex's lungs.

'Oxygen saturation's down to seventy percent,' he said quietly. 'We're in a "can't intubate, can't oxygenate" situation. Have you ever assisted with a surgical cricothyroidotomy?'

'No.' Lisa held his gaze. 'Do you want me to find Tim? Or Peter?'

'There's no time.' Hugh hadn't broken the gaze either. 'You can do this. I'll talk you through it.'

And, within what felt like seconds, when they were both gloved and Hugh had unrolled another kit, that was exactly what he was doing as he palpated the front of Alex's neck around his Adam's apple after swabbing it with antiseptic.

'I can feel the thyroid cartilage here and this is the cricoid cartilage. I'm aiming for the space between them, where the membrane is, and I've got a good grip on it all so nothing moves.'

With his free hand, Hugh picked up a scalpel and made first a vertical incision and then a horizontal one. Because Alex was now deeply unconscious and this was such an urgent situation, there was no time or need for local anaesthesia but Lisa found herself holding her breath at Hugh's confident, swift movements.

'I can feel the "pop" so I know I'm in the trachea now.' Even his voice sounded calm. 'I'm going to put my finger in when I take the scalpel out but what I need you to do is pick up that tracheal hook, put it at the top end of the incision and retract everything for me.'

Lisa had never been this hands on in such a dramatic invasion procedure but, amazingly, her hand wasn't shaking and she had no problem following Hugh's clear instructions. She watched as he widened the incision, inserted a bougie as a guide for the endotracheal tube that followed and then inflated the balloon around the end of the tube that would help secure it. He attached the Ambu bag to the tube and squeezed it.

'Good chest rise,' he said quietly. 'I'll have a listen to be sure and then we can take that hook out and secure the tube properly.'

Lisa could tell that the tube had been correctly placed because the concentration of oxygen in Alex's blood was already increasing and his heart rate slowing a little. They had got through a crisis that could have killed an otherwise healthy young person and, when Hugh looked up and smiled at Lisa, while he was still listening to lung sounds with his stethoscope, she knew that he was just as happy as she was.

They had done this together. She could hear other people arriving in the medical centre now, with rapid footsteps coming towards the treatment room, but it was Lisa and Hugh who had done the hard work here. They were the only ones to have shared that rising tension, background alarm of the ticking clock of a limited amount of time available and the nail-biting stress of a dramatic procedure to deal with it. So they were the only ones who got to share this moment of relief. Joy, even.

Along with something else. A knowledge that they could work together this closely under extreme circumstances. That they could trust each other. That they were in exactly the same place when it came to how much they cared about their patients and how hard they were prepared for a fight for something that really mattered. The moment of connection was only a heartbeat before others rushed into the room but the effect lingered as Lisa stepped back to let Peter and Tim close to their patient. It was Tim who was tasked with securing the tube and Peter assisted Hugh in setting up the portable ventilator.

'We'll need transport to the nearest hospital. He'll need intensive care monitoring for a while.'

'Chopper?'

'Possibly. We might be close enough to

shore for a coastguard vessel. I'll get hold of the captain.'

'I can go with him, if he needs an escort,' Tim offered.

Hugh nodded his acknowledgment of the offer but his gaze shifted to Lisa, one eyebrow raised. Was he asking if she wanted that drama? Maybe he was even suggesting that they both go to look after the man who had been a patient they had both been so invested in saving. Suddenly, it felt like the connection they had just forged was strong enough to make Lisa feel flustered. Unsure of which way to jump and it was a well-practised habit to find a safe option as quickly as possible. Ignoring the unspoken invitation was a first step. Removing herself from the situation was the second.

'We'll need more details, won't we?' she said. 'I could go back up to the Lido deck where we found him. They might have found his clothes and his medication. He'll need something more than a swimming suit when they discharge him.'

'Good thinking, Lisa.' It was Peter who

was nodding now. 'We can get Housekeeping to go to his cabin and pack a few things for him as well. I'll get someone to meet you.'

By the time Lisa got back to the medical centre with Alex's suitcase, she found the entire team were ready to escort their patient up to helipad at the very bow of the ship.

'None of us need to go with him.' Hugh had a clipboard in his hands and must have been working fast to have written up what looked like a very detailed report. 'They're sending an intensive care doctor and a paramedic to take him back.'

'Come and watch,' Janet said. 'It doesn't happen that often and it's pretty exciting, especially in the middle of the night.'

'Does the ship have to stop?'

'It's already slowing down but I've seen them land even in fairly big seas when the ship is going fast. If it's too dangerous to land, they'll winch the patient up. They're amazing.'

It was an opportunity not to be missed. Lisa followed the entourage and waited with them to watch as the helicopter got close enough to glow in the floodlit area of the helipad located right at the bow of the ship, overlooked by the bridge, as it hovered and very slowly sank until its skids were on the deck. Two of the French crew ducked their heads beneath the still whirring blades of the aircraft and came to meet Hugh, who was standing at the head of Alex's stretcher, holding the clipboard, raising his voice to give a verbal handover to the new health professionals in charge.

'Bonjour, messieurs. Voici Alex, qui a eu une réaction anaphylactique sévère...'

The fact that Hugh was doing the handover in French was not only astonishing, it completely took Lisa's breath away. That he was already such a charming and good-looking man had been quite enough to deal with in terms of being happy to keep herself at a safe distance. That he seemed to be at ease speaking what had to be the most beautiful language on earth took his attractiveness to another level and, on top of that, there was now that moment of connection they'd shared tonight that made Lisa think that the social planets they inhabited might not be that far apart after all.

Minutes later, she also had to wonder whether the butterflies that had taken over her stomach were due solely to the excitement of standing here as the helicopter lifted off and swung away right in front of her, the beat of its rotors vibrating right through her body. It was quite possible that these unfamiliar sensations had even more to do with the man who was standing right beside her.

It was no wonder that Lisa found it impossible to go back to bed and try to sleep after the tension and excitement of the last few hours. Even though it was nearly three a.m. she decided she needed to go and walk off the adrenaline or whatever it was that was still bubbling in her veins and making her brain race in an endless loop of reliving those fraught minutes of working to save Alex's life. The beat of fear when she'd believed she was facing the challenge alone. The relief when Hugh had arrived. That feeling of someone moving close enough to touch her soul when they'd shared the joy of success and, possibly the most disconcerting recurrent thought, how she'd felt when she'd heard him speaking French so fluently.

Yes…that very odd, melting sensation that was happening every time that part of the loop resurfaced was the best reason of all to go for a brisk walk and get some fresh air outside.

Lisa headed for the stairs that would take her to the deck she wanted that had a running track available. They were right beside a set of elevators and the doors on one slid open as she walked past. She heard the giggle of an obviously inebriated woman and she probably would have heard her voice even if she was halfway up the stairs.

'But you *are* coming to my cabin, aren't you, darling? You promised…'

'Yes, I did. And I will. Oops-a-daisy… I think you'd better hang on a bit more tightly…'

It was the sound of the male voice that made Lisa turn her head and slow her feet enough to count as a long pause. A deep,

sexy voice with that note of muted amusement she was rather familiar with. She knew
she was staring. She knew her mouth was
gaping and she was probably looking as ap-
palled as she was feeling.

For one long, horrified moment she held
Hugh Patterson's gaze. And then she all but
fled up the stairs because, quite honestly, she
couldn't get away fast enough. Not that she
had any intention of trying to analyse why
she felt so…disappointed? Because she suspected that there might be a corner of her
mind that could justifiably taunt her with
the notion that she was jealous.

Oh…*man*…

It had been all too obvious what Lisa Phillips had been thinking when she'd seen him
holding up that drunk woman in the lift. She
probably wouldn't believe him if he told her
that he'd found the woman rather too worse
for wear when he'd gone back to the bar on
the Lido deck to reassure the staff who'd
been so worried about Alex, and he'd offered
to make sure she got safely back to her own

cabin. What was his nurse still doing up, anyway? He had the excuse of having been waiting for an update from the hospital that had taken their patient and then spending time with the staff on the Lido deck, but Lisa should have been in bed long before now.

As if he'd ever take advantage of an inebriated passenger. Or any passenger, for that matter. Okay, it was not unpleasant to have an endlessly changing number of beautiful women who were often remarkably uninhibited in advertising that they'd like to add to their holiday pleasures by including a dalliance with him but he very rarely had any desire to do more than a bit of harmless flirting.

He'd practically been a monk, for heaven's sake—apart from that first cruise when he'd been a passenger and not a crew member, of course, and when he'd needed a lot more than the on-board entertainment to distract himself from the betrayal of the woman he'd believed had loved him as much as he'd loved her. A woman he'd been on the verge of committing to for the rest of his life, in fact.

His friendship with Carlotta, in Barcelona,

was the closest he'd come to in any kind of relationship since then and they both knew that it was no more than a friendship with occasional benefits.

It seemed a bit ironic that the first time he'd seen Lisa she'd been watching him kiss Carlotta and he'd been well aware that she'd been somewhat shocked. Well…she'd looked more than shocked when she'd seen him in the elevator tonight. She'd looked positively disgusted, and the worst thing about that was that a part of Hugh's brain could see himself through her eyes only too easily and… he had to admit, it looked shallow.

He looked like a pleasure-seeker with a job that might provide the occasional medical challenge, as tonight had done, but was mostly delivering a kind of private general practice, catering for an elite group of people who were wealthy enough to take luxury holidays. It was also a job that could obviously provide a playground for unlimited sexual adventures.

Hugh didn't like the thought that Lisa would think so little of him. But, then again, he didn't like the idea that she was judging him either. She knew nothing about why he was here or how much satisfaction this job could deliver on a regular basis. She was only here for a couple of weeks anyway, so why the hell should it matter *what* she thought?

But it seemed that it did. Having found a female crew member who had helped him get the passenger back to her cabin and taken over the responsibility of getting her into bed and checking on her later, Hugh didn't go straight back to his own cabin. He needed a bit of fresh air, he decided. A moment to take a breath and dismiss whatever unpleasant vibe that look on Lisa's face had left him with.

It was unfortunate that he chose that particular deck to go out onto. Or that his new colleague had still not retired to her cabin and was looking over the railing at the stern of the ship, watching the moonlight sparkle on the impressive foam of the wake stretching back into the inky darkness of the sea. It was even more unfortunate that, when she finally noticed him walking in her direction, she chose to try and make some sort of negative comment about his sexual prowess.

'That was quick,' she said. She sounded surprised but there was a smile tugging at the corners of her mouth, as if the idea of him being terrible in bed was somehow unexpected but amusing.

'Excuse me?' Hugh stopped. He took a breath, trying to put a lid on how defensive he was feeling, but the lid didn't quite fit. 'I take it that you're assuming I jumped into bed with the passenger you saw me with?'

'The invitation was obviously there.'

'And you think I would have been unable to resist? That I sleep with every woman who offers invitations for sex even if they're not sober or if it might jeopardise the position I hold here?'

Her gaze slid away from his. 'It's none of my business,' she said. At least she had the grace to sound uncomfortable. She might even be blushing, although it was hard to tell in this light, but Hugh wasn't about to let her off that lightly. For some inexplicable reason this mattered.

Maybe that was because he was feeling something other than defensive. Something like disappointment? Working with Lisa tonight and especially that moment when they'd both acknowledged how amazing it was to know that you'd saved someone's life had given Hugh a feeling of connection with a woman that was different from anything he'd ever experienced before.

A chink in his armour even, where he could feel what it must be like to be with someone you could really trust. Someone who could share the important things of life—for either celebration or encouragement to conquer. And maybe he had felt that way because he'd seen himself in a big brother role, which gave Lisa the status of family—someone it was safe to care about.

But she was judging him and his lifestyle now and any glimmer from that chink in his protective armour was nowhere to be seen. Lisa wasn't family. She was a stranger and, while she might be damned good at her job, she was uptight to the point of being a prude.

'At least I know how to relax occasionally and enjoy myself,' he heard himself saying. 'What's *your* problem, Lisa?'

'I haven't got one.'

She sounded as defensive as he had been feeling and Hugh could see that her hands were gripping the railing so tightly her knuckles were white. Was she *scared* of something? Hugh contemplated the ship's wake for a long moment and he could actually feel his negative thoughts getting washed away and disappearing into the night. There was something vulnerable about Lisa. She was the one who needed encouragement right now, even if she didn't realise it. He injected a teasing note into his voice as he turned to lean his back against the railing so he could watch Lisa's reaction.

'Are you a virgin?' he asked.

That shocked expression he'd seen on her face when she'd seen him propping up that passenger in the lift was back again.

'*No*... Of course I'm not.'

'But I'm guessing you don't like sex that much?'

Her breath came out in such an incredulous huff he could hear it over the hum of the engines and the sound of the churning water far below them.

'Just because I don't approve of jumping into bed with total strangers?' Her chin came up. 'I think sex is an important part of a relationship, if you must know. But I also happen to think there are more important things.'

'I'm not talking about a relationship.' Hugh was keeping his tone light. He was curious about how far down the list sex would come on the list of important things in a relationship for her but that could wait for another conversation. Right now, all he wanted to find out was just how tightly this woman kept herself under control.

'I'm just talking about sex,' he added. 'Enjoying a physical activity. Like dancing.' This seemed inspired. Did Lisa ever let herself go enough to dance? 'Do you dance?'

'No.' Lisa was resolutely keeping her gaze

on the endless wake, although he had the feeling that she knew how closely he was watching her.

Hugh could feel a frown line appearing between his eyebrows as he leaned a little closer so that he could lower his voice. 'What about eating some amazing meal? Or drinking champagne? Do you like drinking champagne, Lisa?'

She shrugged. 'I've never tasted real champagne.'

Wow…she'd never tasted a lot of things, it seemed. Hugh's annoyance had long since vanished. He was watching Lisa's profile— the way the wind was playing with that short tumble of waves, the freckles he could see dusting her pale cheeks and that delicious curve at the corners of her mouth that looked like an embryonic smile, even though she was clearly not that happy at the moment.

Hugh leaned even closer. So close he could feel the tickle of a windblown lock of hair touch his forehead.

'What *do* you enjoy, then?' he asked.

He hadn't really intended to use his best

flirtatious tone that he knew women loved. He hadn't actually intended to be this close to Lisa and he certainly hadn't expected the punch in his gut when she turned her head slowly and he found himself so very close to those remarkable eyes. They were a very dark shade of golden brown right now, with the pupils dilating rapidly towards that intriguing dark rim.

Hugh knew exactly what that punch in his gut was telling him. He also knew by Lisa's reaction that she was experiencing the same thing. Whether or not she was prepared to acknowledge that shaft of desire was quite another matter and Hugh knew he should move before she even had the time to think about it. He should step back, say something about it being far too late to be out and about and escape before this odd moment turned into something they might both regret.

Except he left it a split second too late. Just long enough for his gaze to catch something other than the expression in Lisa's eyes. He could see the way her lips were parting… The way the tip of her tongue appeared to touch her bottom lip. It was mesmerising, that's what it was. Hugh was unaware of any movement from either of them but their faces were even closer now. Close enough for their noses to touch as his mouth hovered above hers.

And then their lips touched. So lightly it was no more than a feather-light brush—not dissimilar to the touch of the wind that Hugh could feel caressing the bare skin on his arms and neck as he bent his head. A scrape of a touch that was also similar to a match being struck and it certainly created a flame. It was impossible not to repeat the action and, this time, Hugh could feel the response.

He might have expected Lisa to be shocked. He was shocked himself, to be honest, but it seemed that even that gentlest of touches contained something far too powerful to be resisted. On both sides. There was nothing for it but to *really* kiss her, Hugh decided as he covered her lips with his own and began a conversation that he might have had a thousand times already in his life but he'd never found one quite like this.

Ever...

Oh...dear Lord...

She'd wondered what it might be like to be kissed by this man from the moment she'd first clapped eyes on him kissing another woman. She'd imagined how it might feel. She'd even dreamt about it but she'd had *no* idea, had she?

It wasn't the first time she'd been kissed by any means but it *felt* like it was.

Who knew that there were such infinite variations in pressure and movement that a kiss could feel like listening to the most amazing music with its different notes and rhythms? That closing your eyes would only intensify other senses and there'd never been anything that tasted like Hugh's mouth and that the silky glide of his tongue against hers would trigger a sensation that felt like the inside of her whole body was melting...

She could feel the absolute control that Hugh had but she could sense the strength behind it and she wanted more. So much more. If a kiss with this man could be like this, what would sex be like?

Any judgement she might have had about people on cruise ships who were intent on finding as much pleasure as possible in the shortest amount of time were disappearing— getting buried under the weight of curiosity. No...make that a kind of desire that Lisa had never, ever experienced before. Hugh hadn't been that far off the mark, had he, when he'd suggested that she didn't like sex that much? She'd never been kissed like this, though. Or felt desire that was more like a desperate need to discover something she might otherwise miss out on for the rest of her life.

It was a subtle change in the engine noise beneath them that finally broke that kiss. Or perhaps it was a need for more oxygen because Lisa knew she was breathing far more rapidly than normal as they pulled apart. Her lips were still parted as well, and her eyes drifted open to find her gaze locking onto Hugh's.

His smile grew slowly. 'I take it back,' he said.

'Take what back?' The thought that he was already regretting that kiss was like a shower of cold water in her face.

'Thinking you were so uptight,' Hugh said. 'Where did you learn to kiss like that, Lisa Phillips?'

She couldn't say anything. Because she'd have to admit that she'd never learned to kiss like that until he'd taught her? Or because she was processing the fact that he'd considered her to be uptight? Lisa could feel herself taking a step back to create some more distance between them.

Was Hugh laughing at her? She couldn't let him know that that kiss had, quite possibly, been life-changing for her when it was probably no more than an everyday occurrence for Hugh. He'd think she was immature as well as uptight, wouldn't he? Had he just been amusing himself all along by kissing her in the first place? Or…and it was a horrible thought…had she been the one who had initiated that kiss? Lisa could feel her cheeks reddening in one of her hated blushes so she turned away so that she could catch the breeze on her face.

'We're slowing down.' Hugh broke a silence that was on the verge of becoming really awkward moments later as the engine noise dropped another note. 'We can't be that far away from docking. I expect we'll have a busy clinic in the morning. When most of the passengers have gone ashore, it gives a lot of the crew a chance to visit us.'

He was talking like her boss, which prompted Lisa to shift her gaze to catch his again. Was he dismissing that kiss as something that shouldn't have happened between people who had to work together? Or was he warning her that it couldn't go any further? It was more like there was a question to be seen in his eyes than a warning, however. Maybe he was wondering if he should say something about that kiss? Or was he waiting for an indication from her that she'd enjoyed it as much as he had? That she wasn't that "uptight" after all?

Well…she didn't have to prove anything.

And she didn't want to talk about it either—
certainly not with someone who thought sex
was just something to enjoy as a physical activity, like dancing or drinking champagne.
She'd already let Hugh know how much she
disapproved of people who simply jumped
into bed with each other for no other reason
than giving in to lust.

Okay, she might have just gained a disturbing new insight into how it could easily
happen but, now that she'd had a moment to
catch her breath, she could remember that
she wasn't that type of person herself. That
she knew it was dangerous to break rules or
step too far outside the boundaries of what
you knew was the right thing to do. The safe
thing.

Maybe what Hugh was really asking was if
she'd like to pretend the kiss had never happened. Or that it was no big deal—which it
obviously wasn't for someone like Hugh. It
was the first thing she'd ever seen him doing,
after all. Perhaps he'd mentioned work because it was a safer topic and a place where
they had discovered a professional connec-

tion and that was absolutely something Lisa could use as a life raft when her head was such a whirlpool of jumbled sensations and emotions she was in danger of drowning. She grabbed hold of it.

'And it's late,' she added briskly, turning away. 'Don't know about you but I need some sleep before I turn up for work. See you in the morning, Hugh.'

CHAPTER FOUR

HOW THE HELL had that happened, exactly?

Okay, he'd been pushing her a bit after being irritated by that unimpressed comment that he had interpreted as judgement on his performance in bed. Deliberately being in her personal space as well as he'd prodded that barrier Lisa seemed to have between herself and the good things in life, but he'd certainly never expected it to end in a kiss. He hadn't even been attracted to her, given that she was so not his type. Was that what had made that kiss seem so different? Why it had haunted his dreams in the few snatched hours of sleep he'd managed later and why it was still lurking in the perimeter of his consciousness this morning?

Hugh arrived early at the medical centre, despite his lack of sleep, but moving around his familiar environment as he checked that everything had been thoroughly cleaned and restocked in the wake of managing their dramatic case of Alex's respiratory arrest due to anaphylaxis in the early hours of this morning, he was aware of an unfamiliar tension.

He might not understand how that kiss had happened exactly but there was no getting away from the fact that it *had* happened and now it felt like it was going to be more than a little awkward working with Lisa. Most women he knew would be happy to either dismiss that kiss as fun but naughty, given they had to work together, or to enjoy a bit of sexual tension and have fun playing with it for a while. But Lisa wasn't like any of the women he knew and Hugh wasn't confident he would know how to respond to a different, less relaxed reaction.

Sure enough, when she arrived a few minutes before morning surgery was due to begin, she avoided any direct eye contact with him when he gave her a friendly greeting and said that he hoped she'd had enough sleep, given her extended working hours last night.

She merely nodded, still not meeting his gaze as she reached for a stethoscope to hook around her neck. 'Shall I set up in the second consulting room to do the initial obs?'

'Yes, please.' So she was going to pretend the kiss had never happened? That was a bit "head in the sand", but he could go along with that. And it was always useful to get an idea of what a patient was presenting with, along with baseline observations that let him know whether they had any signs of infection like a fever or any problems with their blood pressure or heart rhythm. A competent nurse could also deal with minor stuff herself, like dressing a burn or closing a small laceration with sticky strips or glue.

It was a walk-in clinic that didn't require appointments and the knowledge, based on experience, that they might be very busy for the next couple of hours should have been enough to focus Hugh's attention completely on his job.

Except it wasn't quite enough. He was

watching Lisa from the corner of his eye as she moved swiftly around the medical centre for the next few minutes, collecting supplies like the plastic sheaths for the tip of the tympanic thermometer, a new roll of graph paper for the ECG monitor and dressing supplies and antiseptic ointments that might be needed to deal with minor injuries that didn't need a doctor's attention. How hard was she finding it to pretend that the kiss hadn't happened?

Was she thinking about it as much as he was? Those unwanted flashes of memory that were strong enough to interfere with anything else he might be trying to focus on? Did she have the same, disturbing idea that it could be tempting to do it again or was she avoiding even looking at him directly because she really was wishing it had never happened in the first place?

He found himself listening in from the treatment room as he made sure the electronic equipment like the X-ray machine was turned on and ready for use, when Janet arrived to help with the surgery by manning the reception area and triaging to get the most important cases seen first.

'Tim's been telling me about all the excitement last night. Can't believe something like that happened when I'm not even on call.'

'It was a memorable night, that's for sure. Possibly a once-in-a-lifetime experience.'

Hugh flicked another switch to turn the steriliser on. Was Lisa making a reference to the case...or the kiss? Not that it mattered, because maybe he agreed with her—on both counts.

'You could be right. I've never seen a cricothyroidotomy done on land, let alone at sea.'

'I'd never seen one done either and I've worked in ED a lot. It was amazing. *Hugh* was amazing. He saved that guy's life...'

'*We* saved that guy's life.' Hugh couldn't eavesdrop any more when he was the subject of the conversation.

Perhaps it was because she was startled by his sudden appearance or the genuine compliment he was offering that Lisa finally looked at him properly and something in

Hugh's gut did an odd little flip as her gaze met his. The last time he'd seen those eyes had been very close up indeed...

'Lisa was first on the scene,' he added, 'and I couldn't have handled his airway later without her excellent assistance.'

'So he actually arrested?' Janet was open-mouthed.

'Close enough. His oxygen saturation got down to below seventy percent at one stage and he was unconscious.'

'Wow...'

'Have you had any update on his condition?'

Lisa shifted her gaze swiftly as he looked back to answer her question. The way she was biting her lower lip was another sign that she was finding any interaction between them awkward this morning and that had the effect of making whatever that was in Hugh's gut flip back the other way. Yep... this was awkward all right and Hugh was aware of a beat of another, unfamiliar emotion.

Guilt? He'd imagined himself in a big

brother kind of role with Lisa, hadn't he? Well…nobody would trust him to take on that kind of role again, would they? Had he really asked her if she was a virgin? And suggested that maybe she didn't like sex? How insulting had that been? Plus, he'd told her how uptight he'd thought she was as well and that had been an unkind thing to say. No wonder Lisa had backed off so fast. She probably wasn't looking forward to working with him at all and he couldn't blame her.

'Alex is fine,' he said aloud. 'They monitored him in Intensive Care for the rest of the night but everything had settled by the time I spoke to someone an hour or so ago. They're going to patch up his neck, give him a course of steroids for a couple of days and have advised him to wear a medic alert bracelet and make sure he has his auto-injector within reach at all times. He should be back on board before we sail this evening.'

A late sailing, Hugh remembered, turning to head into his consulting room as Janet moved to open the doors to their first patients. And after this morning's surgery he had the day to himself in one of his favourite parts of the world, which was just what he needed. A chance to relax and soak up some of the very best things in life. The kind of things that Lisa didn't seem to be at all familiar with. That he'd thought he could help her discover. Maybe he could try and step back into that helpful role.

He turned back. 'What are you going to do with your first onshore leave, Lisa?'

If nothing else, he could provide some recommendations for things she could see or do and that might get them past this awkwardness.

'I'm not sure.' Lisa's gaze skittered away from his again. 'One of the team on the excursions desk told me about a walk that was lovely around the Cap d'Antibes but what I'd really love to see is one of the medieval towns.'

'Get up to Eze, if you can. It's an outstanding example of a medieval village. Or St Paul de Vence, although that could still be pretty crowded on a lovely day like this. It's a shame we won't finish in time for you to tag along with one of the organised bus tours. They're always keen to have someone from our team available as medical cover but a taxi probably wouldn't be too expensive. Less than fifty euros, probably.'

The expression on Lisa's face suggested that their ideas of what wasn't too expensive were poles apart. She was the one to turn away this time but he caught the hint of smile that felt like an acknowledgement of his effort to restore their working relationship to its former amicability. Not that it seemed to have worked particularly well.

'I expect I'll just take a walk around Villefranche sur Mer from where the tender boat drops us,' she said. 'Or I can find the bus that goes into Nice. I'll explore the old town and then find somewhere lovely for a late lunch. I'm sure it will be gorgeous.'

Oh...*help*...

The first time Lisa had been in this reception area and had realised that she was going to be working with Hugh, she hadn't been able to dismiss the memory of having seen him kissing that leggy blonde woman.

Now she was totally unable to dismiss the memory of having been kissed herself. And it was so much more than merely a thought. She could actually *feel* it happening again. The soft press of his lips on hers. The taste of his mouth. The fierce lick of desire that sent an electric buzz to every cell in her body and made her knees feel distinctly weak.

Biting her bottom lip hard enough to hurt helped. So did avoiding any more than a split second of eye contact. Even better was being able to focus on the patients that started arriving within the next few minutes. Hugh had been right—they were in for a very busy few hours and, best of all, there was plenty for Lisa to do in her consulting room and she wasn't being asked to assist Hugh in any way.

An hour in and she was starting to feel a lot more confident that they could continue working together without the awkwardness of that kiss hanging in the air between them.

A purely professional exchange presented no problems at all after the first couple.

'This is Elaine.' Lisa handed the clipboard to Hugh as she took her tenth patient into his consulting room. 'She's running a fever of thirty-nine point six, has frequency and pain on urination and the dipstick test was positive for blood in her urine.'

It would be a quick consult for Hugh to double check the history and any other health issues that Elaine had and then prescribe the antibiotics and other medications to ease the discomfort of a urinary tract infection for their patient.

Jeff, the next patient, only needed a certificate to be signed by Hugh to give him a day away from his job as a kitchen hand.

'It's a second degree burn but the blisters are still intact,' Lisa told him. 'I've cleaned it, put antibiotic cream on and a non-stick gauze dressing and I've told Jeff to come back tomorrow for a dressing change so that I can make sure it's not infected. If it's looking okay, I think he'll be able to work as long as he wears gloves and keeps it dry.'

Hugh scrawled his signature on the certificate. 'How's the waiting room looking?'

'Still quite full. I've got someone with chest pain to do an ECG on now, but he's a dancer in one of the cabaret acts and I suspect he's pulled a muscle.'

'It should start to slow down soon.' Hugh handed back the piece of paper and smiled at Lisa. 'You're doing a great job,' he told her. 'Thanks...'

She tucked the praise away as she went back to Jeff to give him his final instructions on how to look after his burn injury today and sort out an appointment for a dressing change tomorrow morning. Hugh's words made her feel good, she decided, but they hadn't undermined the relief of stepping back into the purely professional interactions between herself and her boss. If anything, they were giving what had happened in the early hours of today a dreamlike quality— as if that kiss couldn't possibly have happened for real.

The final patient that came in turned out to be the real test of whether things were back to normal. A tall, brusque Scotsman in his fifties, he was reluctant to admit to having anything wrong.

'But if it gets any worse, I'm not going to be able to do any more of these tours, Nurse,' he said as he limped from the waiting room. 'I can barely put any weight on my foot now.'

His anxious wife was by his side. 'We're supposed to be doing a tour of St Jean Cap Ferrat that includes lunch at that amazing hotel that was in a movie we saw recently. The *Abolutely Fabulous* one? It would be such a shame to miss out.'

Lisa had a look at the sole of the man's foot. He had a reddened area just below his middle toes that could be a deep blister.

'Let me just run a couple of checks and then we'll get the doctor to have a look.' Lisa wrapped a blood pressure cuff around his arm. 'You haven't been doing a lot of walking in a new pair of shoes, have you? Going barefoot more than usual? Could you have had an injury that you might not have taken much notice of, like a stone bruise?'

She went in with her patient to give handover to Hugh a few minutes later. 'This is Gordon,' she told him. 'He's presenting with nine out of ten pain when he tries to put any weight on the ball of his left foot. Vital signs are all normal. He had an injury two weeks ago when he was replacing boards on his deck and fell through a rotten part but he was treated in his local ED and discharged.'

'Oh? What did they do for treatment?'

'Cleaned out a small cut but it wasn't anything to worry about.' Gordon shook his head, dismissing the incident. 'They X-rayed my foot, too, in case I'd broken something but they said it all looked fine. They gave me a tetanus shot and some antibiotics.'

'And it's only started to get painful again now?'

'It's been sore ever since.' It was Gordon's wife who spoke. 'He's just been putting a brave face on it but when he got up this morning it was suddenly a whole lot worse. He almost fell over.'

Lisa had been about to leave Hugh to deal

with his patient and go and finish up her own paperwork but he caught her gaze.

'Could you set up the treatment room for us, please?' he asked. 'I think we'll have a look with the ultrasound.'

'Why would you want to do that?' Gordon's wife echoed Lisa's first thought. 'I thought ultrasounds were just for when you were pregnant.'

Lisa had seen that kind of smile on Hugh's face many times already but this time she noticed the crinkles around his eyes as well. It wasn't that he was making fun of a layperson's lack of medical knowledge in any way. This smile held understanding rather than amusement and it was also reassuring. Lisa knew that the people in front of him would be confident that he cared about them. That he was doing what he believed might help.

'There are some things that don't show up on X-rays,' he told them. 'It could be that there's something in your foot, like a piece of glass or a splinter.'

Sure enough, there was something to be

seen on the screen as Hugh gently examined Gordon's foot.

'The entry wound's healed over now,' Hugh warned. 'We'll need to do a bit of minor surgery to open it up and see what we can find. Are you happy for us to do that or would you like a referral to an emergency department of a local hospital?'

'I'd rather you did it, Doc. That way we can get it over with and we might make our posh lunch after all.'

'Oh…' His wife didn't look so happy. 'I can't watch. Not if there's going to be blood…'

Hugh's smile reappeared. 'Don't worry,' he said. 'We'll get Janet to make you a nice cup of tea while you wait. Lisa and I have got this covered. We're the A team, aren't we?'

Reopening a wound to explore it for the presence of a foreign body was a walk in the park compared to making an opening in someone's neck to establish an emergency airway. Lisa found herself smiling back at Hugh in total agreement. They most definitely did have this covered and it could prove to be a very satisfying end to their morning clinic. Even better, it seemed that the awkwardness had finally evaporated.

This was fun.

Minor surgery was an unexpected finale to an ordinary clinic but Hugh really was enjoying himself. He'd already known that Lisa was someone that he could rely on in a tense, emergency situation but this time he could relax and appreciate her skilled assistance even more. As he filled a syringe with local anaesthetic, he watched her setting up everything he could need on a tray and then swabbing the skin of Gordon's foot and arranging sterile drapes to protect the area.

'This is going to hurt, isn't it?' Gordon's stoic expression slipped a little.

'Not once the local is doing its job,' Hugh assured him. 'Bit of a sting just to start with. Lisa, can you hold Gordon's foot steady, please?

It wasn't the easiest area of the body to be working on and it was frustrating to be able to feel the tip of whatever it was embedded in his patient's foot but be unable to grasp it firmly enough to extract it. Hugh could feel Lisa watching him as he pressed a little deeper into the wound and opened the forceps a little wider. Then he took a grip and held it and this time he could feel something shift. The dark object slowly came out through the skin and just kept coming. With a silent whistle of how impressed he was, Hugh held up an enormous triangular splinter between the teeth of the forceps.

'Look at that.'

He didn't need to tell Lisa to look. She was staring in disbelief that anyone could have been walking around with something that size buried in their foot. Her gaze only had to shift a fraction to catch Hugh's, given that he was watching her reaction, and he wasn't disappointed. Her astonishment morphed into delight. Or maybe it was just professional satisfaction but it didn't matter because just watching the change was a joy. The note of connection might pale in comparison to the satisfaction they'd shared in getting a secure airway into Alex last night but this was significant in its own way because it felt like that awkwardness between himself and Lisa had gone.

She certainly sounded happier. 'You're not going to believe how big this splinter is,' she told Gordon. 'You've been walking around with a log in your foot.'

Hugh showed their patient what he'd pulled out and Gordon grinned. 'That's a piece of my deck, that is. No wonder it was a wee bit sore.'

'I'm going to clean out the wound thoroughly now,' Hugh told him, 'and then we'll get you patched up and bandaged. You might want to keep the weight off your foot as much as you can today but there's no reason you can't go and enjoy your lunch.'

As he intended to enjoy his own. It was nearly two p.m. by the time Hugh had taken one of the tender shuttles to get into the port of Villefranche sur Mer and he was delighted to find that his arrangements for the afternoon were in place. He picked up the keys to the classic car he'd hired, and when the powerful engine of the gunmetal-grey nineteen-sixties E-type Jaguar purred into life a short time later he just smiled and listened to it for a moment, before pulling onto the road.

It was a sparkling blue day with that soft light and warmth that he loved about the French Riviera. He was going to put the roof of this convertible down and drive up towards the mountains and one of his most favourite restaurants ever. He might even indulge in a glass of the best champagne they had on ice.

Lisa Phillips had never tasted champagne…

The thought came from nowhere but with an intensity that let him imagine exactly what she might look like when she did taste it for the first time. He would see that surprise in her eyes and be able to watch it shift and grow and light up her whole face with the pleasure of something new and delicious. Kind of like the way he'd seen her satisfaction with her work but better somehow. More like what he'd seen in her eyes after that kiss? Until he'd ruined the moment by telling her how uptight she was.

Why had he done that? It was almost as if he'd been trying to push her away as a form of self-protection but that was ridiculous. Even if Lisa had been completely his type of woman, he had absolute control over how involved he ever got with anyone. He wasn't about to make the mistake of falling in love again.

But, hey…maybe he could bring a bottle of champagne back with him as a way of making up for being a bit of a jerk.

Or…

Maybe there was a way he could not only make it up to Lisa but reassure himself just how in control of his own feelings he was.

He was moving slowly down the street now, towards a new group of people who'd just been ferried from the cruise ship by the tender. Heads were turning to admire the car he was driving but he was focused only on the solitary figure amongst them. Lisa was wearing a pale yellow T-shirt, jeans that were rolled up to mid-calf, and sensible-looking shoes on her feet that would be just right for a lot of walking as she explored the medieval centres of either Villefranche or Nice. She was clutching her shoulder bag as if she expected a pickpocket was already following her and, as Hugh got closer, he saw her pause and look around. He could even see the way she was taking a deep breath as if she might be a little overwhelmed by the prospect of a solo adventure but he could sense her determination as well. She was going to make the most of whatever new experiences were in store for her in the next few hours.

His foot pressed on the brake as he made the decision to go with that flash of inspiration he'd just had. The car was right in front of Lisa as he stopped, and Hugh leaned across the empty passenger seat to open the door. Then he put on what he hoped was his most charming smile.

'Perfect timing,' he said. 'Hop in.'

He couldn't see the expression in her eyes because she was wearing sunglasses but he knew it would be surprised. Possibly shocked. Definitely hesitant.

'You won't regret it.' He caught his own sunglasses, pulling them down enough that she could see his eyes. 'I promise...'

CHAPTER FIVE

LISA OPENED HER mouth to say, *Thanks, but, no thanks.*

Getting back to a working relationship that wasn't full of lingering tension had been hard enough in a professional environment where there'd been any amount of distraction. Spending time with Hugh when he was looking like some celebrity about to do a photo shoot with a vintage sports car would take her right back to square one when she'd just been kissed senseless and hadn't known which way was up.

The words didn't emerge from her mouth, however, because another thought occurred in the same instant. Maybe spending time with Hugh could do the opposite and reassure her that she wasn't someone who ever lost total control. There seemed to be a tacit agreement between them that they were both going to pretend that kiss had never happened after all.

Or…and it was quite hard to silence that naughty whisper in the back of her mind that was wondering if accepting this invitation might actually lead to another one of those extraordinary kisses. Trying to stifle that whisper made Lisa take hold of the open door of the car, ready to push it shut. It would be far less stressful to go exploring on her own.

But now Lisa could actually hear Abby's voice in her ear. And see an imaginary message that could be her sister's response to news of what her day out had involved.

You went driving around on the French Riviera in a vintage sports car with the roof down? With that gorgeous man driving? That's more like it, Lise… Live the dream… and remember…don't send me a photo unless you're with him in some romantic French café. Preferably drinking champagne…

She'd want to know about every detail and it would make her so happy. It might even go a long way towards finally erasing some of that guilt that Abby could never quite let go of—that she had somehow held Lisa back from doing what she really wanted to do in life.

It wouldn't hurt to live the dream just for an afternoon. As a bonus it would give her enough to tell Abby about that her sister wouldn't be able to pick up that Lisa was keeping something to herself as she had no intention to confessing anything about that kiss. Or letting it happen again, despite that whisper. She was in control. She'd learned very early in life to stay in control and not be seduced by anything because that was where danger lay.

If she hadn't stopped to gaze dreamily at that doll in the toyshop window that day, she would have been holding onto Abby's hand far more tightly. The toddler would never have been able to pull away with a gleeful chuckle and run straight onto the road...

Lisa had tested her resolve to stay in control countless times since then. This might be another test for her, but it was nothing more than a friendly gesture on Hugh's part because, clearly, he'd already dismissed as unimportant what had led to their awkwardness this morning. Or maybe it was even an apology that it had happened in the first place? If Lisa declined the offer, that awkwardness might be there again the next time they had to work together and she didn't want that to happen. The hand Lisa had been about to use to push the door of this extraordinary car shut pulled it further open instead and she settled herself onto the smooth, red leather of the passenger seat.

'Hold on to your hat,' Hugh told her. 'You're about to get blown away.'

He wasn't wrong. Lisa was blown away by far more than the wind in her hair. It seemed that Hugh knew these mountains and their villages like the back of his hand and Lisa was whisked from one amazing view to another until they finally stopped, hours later, in a walled, medieval town that sat high on a hilltop with what looked like a view of the entire Côte d'Azur. Ancient stone walls gave way to rippling acres of forest and, in the misty distance, the deep, deep blue of the Mediterranean. The same stone was under-foot on the terrace of the restaurant Hugh took her to. Vines scrambled overhead to provide shade and frame the view from what had to be the best table available. Lisa shook her head.

'So, is this what usually happens when you rock up in a car like this? You get the corner table with the best view? Even if you're with someone who's wearing jeans and whose hair must look like a complete bird's nest after being out in the wind like that?'

Hugh just laughed. 'You look great,' he told her. 'This is a very relaxed place and they only care about providing the best food and wine. Plus...' He winked at Lisa. 'I booked this particular table. I've been here before. Several times.'

Lisa could believe that. She could also be-lieve that he hadn't been here alone on his past visits and, without warning, she was

aware of a beat of something that felt like...
envy? Jealousy, even?

No. How ridiculous was that? She was
only here as a colleague of Hugh's but, even
if she had been here in a far more intimate
capacity as his date, it would be stupid to
feel jealous of other women in this man's
life. There must have been dozens of them in
the past and there would no doubt be dozens
more in the future because Hugh obviously
liked to play hard. He loved dining out and
dancing. Champagne and...sex...

Oh, *help*...

Lisa could feel her cheeks heating up.
Looking around for a distraction—any distraction—she found herself watching the
maître d' of the restaurant approaching with
a white cloth over his arm, a bottle in one
hand and two fluted glasses in the other. A
waiter was following with an ice bucket.

A short time later, Lisa found herself holding her very first glass of real French champagne.

'Chin-chin.' Hugh held up his glass. He
took a sip of the wine but he was watching

Lisa over the rim of the glass. Waiting to see her reaction?

She closed her eyes as the bubbles seemed to explode on her tongue and then almost evaporate before she could swallow the icy liquid. As her eyes flew open in astonishment she saw amusement dancing in Hugh's steady gaze.

'I knew you'd look like that,' he murmured. 'Tastes nice, doesn't it?'

'Unbelievable.' Lisa took another sip and then she had to reach into her bag for her phone. 'Sorry,' she muttered. 'I hate it when people take photos of what they're eating or drinking but Abby's not going to believe this without some proof.'

It was exactly the photo she'd requested, wasn't it? The romantic café. The "cute doctor". The champagne.

'Abby?'

'My sister. Well, she's my half-sister, actually, but we're…um…really close. And I know how much she would love this place.'

'You'll have to come back one day, then,

now that you know where it is. You can bring your sister.'

How amazing would that be? Lisa would give anything for Abby to have the joy she'd had today of cruising mountain roads in a spectacular car, exploring cobbled streets and vibrant marketplaces and cooling off in the shadows of an ancient cathedral or two. How much harder would it be to do that in a wheelchair, though? Lisa had to blink to clear the sting at the back of her eyes as she took a photo of the frosty flute beside the bottle of what she suspected was a very expensive—probably vintage—champagne. Hugh had already told her, politely but firmly, as they'd come into the restaurant that she was here at his invitation and that this was his treat and he would be highly offended if she offered to pay for any of it.

'Let me take one of you with the glass in your hand.' Hugh reached for her phone and Lisa blinked again, held her glass up as if she was toasting Abby and sent a silent message to her sister.

Here I am... Living the dream...

At least it would be easy to convince her sister that she wasn't on a date with Hugh. Who would go out on a date in a T-shirt and jeans?

She needed to take a picture of the view as well. She didn't let embarrassment stop her taking some of their food either. She wanted to capture every detail for Abby, including the beautifully presented salad Niçoise she had ordered, the steam rising from the rame-kin of the boeuf bourguignon that had been Hugh's choice—even the basket piled with sliced baguette.

'So...' Hugh filled Lisa's glass again when he had mopped up the last of his sauce with torn pieces of the crusty bread. 'Tell me about your sister. She must be younger than you, yes?'

'What makes you say that?'

'Well...you're so well organised and you like being in charge.' The corner of Hugh's mouth twitched, as though he was supress-ing a smile. 'I can imagine you being a bossy big sister.'

Was it a magical side-effect of champagne

that made that sound like a compliment? Or maybe it was Hugh's smile.

'I'm six years older,' she admitted. 'It was the perfect age to get a baby sister to help look after and...'

'And?' The prompt from Hugh fell into a sudden silence.

Lisa almost told him. That she'd had to take sole responsibility for Abby on so many occasions that it was like she had been another mother for that tiny baby. That she hadn't done a very good job of it either, because it was her fault that Abby was now facing challenges that would mean it would be so much more difficult for her to end up in a place like this. In a mountain village in France. Drinking real champagne...

She took another mouthful.

'And I love her to bits,' she added quietly. 'I'm missing her and I'm worried about her, to be honest.'

'Why?'

'We've been living together for her whole life but she's just moved into a university hostel and I know that she's going to be fine and that she can cope perfectly well without me. She's amazing, in fact, so I have to get over worrying about her but…'

But Hugh was frowning. 'If Abby's six years younger than you, that makes her… what…about twenty-four?' His gaze was focused intently on Lisa and she could almost see his clever brain putting pieces of a puzzle together. 'Is she…okay?'

'She got badly injured being hit by a car when she was nearly two.' There was no need to tell Hugh that it had been her fault and she'd never stop hating herself for that moment of carelessness. 'She's been in a wheelchair ever since,' she added. 'And she's always needed me. We went to live with our grandmother when Mum died a couple of years later.' Again, Lisa held back on the more sordid detail that her mother's death had been due to an overdose. 'Gran had some health issues of her own so she couldn't really manage the kind of round-the-clock care Abby needed. We always had some help but I did as much as possible myself.' Lisa took a deep breath and reached for her glass of wine again.

'Sorry... I don't usually talk about this stuff. I guess I'm missing Abby because this is the longest time we've ever been apart.' She found a smile. 'I only took this job because she talked me into it. She thought it all sounded very romantic and that it was time I had some fun.'

'And are you?' Hugh was watching her again. 'Having fun?'

Lisa couldn't read his expression but it seemed...serious. Not in that focused, professional kind of way when they were working together. Not in that flirting kind of way, like the first time he'd ever looked at her, and it was definitely not in that intense *I'm about to kiss you* kind of way. This was... just different. A new side of Hugh.

'You don't really think about "having fun", do you?' he added quietly. 'I think that maybe you've always been too busy worrying about and looking after other people to worry about yourself.'

It was a look of respect, that's what it was.

Understanding, perhaps, of how much Lisa had sacrificed along the way, from the small things like not going to play with friends after school because she'd needed to get home and help look after her little sister to being excused from school trips that would take her away from home and even her career choice, because if she'd wanted to follow her first dream to become a doctor she would have had to go away to medical school. Nursing training had been available in her own city.

That Hugh might get how hard some of those decisions had been and respect her for making them made Lisa suddenly feel an enormous pride in everything she'd done. For all those sacrifices she had made—and was still making—in order to be there for her sister. Unjustified pride, perhaps, given that it had been her fault in the first place but it was a lovely feeling, nonetheless. There was something else in his gaze as well...was he feeling sad on her behalf? She needed to reassure him. To reassure herself at the same time, or maybe it was to disguise a flash of guilt that he was only thinking so well of her because he didn't know the whole truth?

'Today has been so much fun,' she told Hugh. 'It's quite likely the best day of my life so far.'

His smile was one of pride. 'There you go. All you needed was the example of an expert. And I'm sorry I said that you were uptight. It's not true, by the way.' He took the bottle from its bed of ice again. 'Uptight people don't love champagne.' He reached for her glass. 'And you'll need to finish this because I'm driving soon. I'd better get us back to the ship before it sails.'

Lisa made a face as she took her glass again. 'Tough job,' she murmured, 'but I guess someone's gotta do it.'

Hugh laughed. 'I like you, Lisa Phillips,' he said. 'We might be total opposites but that doesn't mean we can't be friends, does it?'

They *were* total opposites. Hugh indulged in pleasure of all kinds and Lisa had learned to sacrifice anything that could interfere with what was most important in her life—keeping her sister safe. But Hugh could afford to indulge without any guilt, not only because he could obviously afford it financially— going by the personal information that patient with the migraine had revealed—but more because he didn't have anyone depending on him, did he? He was free to enjoy everything and, today, he'd given Lisa her first taste of that kind of life.

And it had been utterly amazing. It wasn't hard to return his smile. 'How could I not be friends with the person who introduced me to French champagne?'

'My work is done.' Hugh leaned back in his chair. 'If only everything in life could be sorted so easily.'

Friends.

It had been hard to persuade Abby that that was all there was to her relationship with Hugh after she sighed over the romantic photos of that mountaintop café.

'Nothing happened? Really? Not even a kiss?'

'Not even a kiss.' Lisa could sound sincere because they were only discussing the

French outing, not what had happened the night before. 'Or not a real one, that is. We were running late by the time we got back and we only just caught the last tender so we were laughing about it all and then we kind of had a hug to say goodnight and he kissed me on the cheek.'

'Aha! There's still time, then. Sounds like a perfect first date to me.'

'Except that it wasn't a date. Now, tell me what's going on with you. You had your test today, didn't you?'

And fortunately Abby was too excited over the news that she'd not only passed her driver's licence test but had been accepted onto the wheelchair basketball team to try and pry any more information out of her big sister.

'Oh, and I've got my first real, hands-on session with a patient tomorrow, to practise what we've been learning about wound care and splinting. My case is a guy who broke three fingers in a rugby game. I can't wait. I'm going to feel like I'm a huge step closer to being a real hand therapist.'

'Good luck with that. I'll look forward to hearing how it went. We'll be docking near Rome so reception might be good enough for a video call. Ring me when you're all done for the day. I'll be on duty but if I can't take the call I'll ring you back later, okay?'

Lisa did miss Abby's call the following evening. Even if she'd been aware of her phone ringing, she wouldn't have even been able to fish it out of her pocket. She was running at the time, helping Tim the paramedic push the resuscitation trolley that was kept ready to deal with any sudden collapse that could be due to a cardiac arrest. Hugh was already on scene because he happened to be eating in the same restaurant as the man who had simply fallen sideways off his chair while he had been waiting for his main course to be served.

'It's the restaurant that caters for passengers who think an evening meal with the ship's officers is a traditional part of their cruising experience,' Tim told her as he hit buttons to try and make the elevator work faster. 'They love an occasion to get really dressed up. Usually older people so it could well be a cardiac arrest. Lucky they've often got a doctor hosting one of the tables. Peter and Hugh take it in turns.'

Hugh was wearing a different kind of uniform, Lisa noticed as they raced into the small restaurant moments later. He still had a white shirt but it was paired with black trousers and jacket and even a tie. There were other people standing around wearing similar formal outfits and she recognised one as the captain of their ship, although she'd only met him briefly and hadn't been invited to have dinner at his table yet. Most of the diners seemed to have left the area but staff were looking after a distraught-looking woman.

The unconscious man lying on the carpeted floor was certainly not one of the older passengers Tim had told her about. This man barely looked any older than the doctor who was kneeling beside him, performing chest compressions. Maybe that was why there was a flash of real relief on his face when

Hugh looked up to see Lisa and Tim arriving with the trolley.

'Take over compressions, will you, Tim? I've been going for more than two minutes.' Hugh pulled at his tie to loosen and remove it as he straightened up and moved to let Tim kneel. He was shrugging out of his jacket as he scrambled to his feet to get the defibrillator off the trolley. Lisa had already turned it on and taken the sticky pads from the pouch on the side.

'Find some laryngeal mask airways, please, Lisa. We'll need the IV kit and the drug roll. You can set up some saline and make sure we've got adrenaline and amiodarone ready to draw up.'

The next few minutes were controlled chaos. Hugh applied the patches while Tim kept up the rapid compressions until he was asked to stop so that they could identify the rhythm on the screen of the defibrillator.

'It's VF.' Hugh nodded. He pushed a button on the machine and the whine of the increasing charge could be heard. 'Okay, everybody clear. This is going to be a single shock at maximum joules.'

Tim put his hands in the air. 'Clear,' he responded.

Lisa wriggled back from where she was on her knees, unrolling the drug pouch. 'I'm clear,' she added.

The whine changed to an alarm. 'Shocking,' Hugh warned.

Their patient's body arced and then flopped back. He made a sound like a groan despite the mask airway that was filling his mouth and the woman, whom Lisa assumed was his wife, cried out in distress from where she was watching the resuscitation efforts.

'You good to continue compressions?' Hugh asked Tim.

'Yep.' Ideally the person doing the compressions should change every two minutes to keep the energy level high and effective but there was too much to do in a very limited time and Lisa was ideally placed to assist Hugh right now. He needed to get an IV line inserted and the first of the drug dosages administered.

'Draw up one milligram of adrenaline, please, Lisa.'

'On it.' Lisa had put everything he needed for putting in an IV line on a towel. She could watch Hugh moving as she located the ampoule of adrenaline, tapped the top to shift any liquid back into the base and then snapped off the tip so that she could fill a syringe. Hugh's movements were swift and sure. He tightened the tourniquet, felt for only a brief instant for a vein and slid the needle and cannula in only seconds later. By the time Lisa had drawn up the drug, he had secured the line and attached a Luer plug. Lisa handed him the syringe, and the ampoule so he could double check that the right drug was being given.

The first dose of adrenaline made no difference to the potentially fatal rhythm of ventricular fibrillation. A dose of amiodarone was administered, also with no effect. A two-minute cycle was ending so another shock was delivered and Hugh and Tim swapped places for compressions and using the bag mask to deliver oxygen.

'Any cardiac history?' Tim asked.

'No. He's forty-six,' Hugh told him. 'Company director from Canada. His name's Carter.'

'Family history?'

'Clear. No history of congenital heart defects or fainting episodes that might suggest an arrhythmia. He passed a medical recently and his blood pressure and cholesterol were fine. This cruise is the honeymoon for his second marriage. That's his new wife over there.'

Lisa glanced over her shoulder at the woman in a silver evening gown who was standing in complete shock, her hands pressed to her mouth. The ship's captain was right beside her and he was looking just as shocked as it became apparent that this wasn't going well.

At twenty minutes into the resuscitation attempt, with their patient now intubated and receiving continuous chest compressions, another dose of amiodarone was added to the repeated doses of adrenaline and repeated shocks but Lisa could see, every time there was a rhythm check, that the wiggly line of fibrillation was getting flatter and flatter.

News of the emergency must have travelled fast because both Peter and Janet arrived at the restaurant. They now had the ship's full medical team involved and they weren't about to give up but, twenty minutes later, when the line on the screen was absolutely flat, Lisa could tell that the doctors were trying to prepare the man's wife for bad news as they explained what they were trying to achieve with their actions as they still continued the attempt to save Carter's life.

'It's a heart attack, isn't it?' she sobbed.

'It's a cardiac arrest,' Hugh told her gently, leaving Peter to carry on as he went to stand beside her. 'A heart attack is when an artery is blocked and blood can't get to the heart. An arrest is when something is disturbing the electrical current that makes the heart beat. It can be caused by a heart attack. More often it's caused by something that interferes with the rhythm.'

'He's…he's not going to be okay, is he?'

'We've done everything we can,' Hugh said, his tone sombre. 'We've shocked him and used all the drugs we can to try and correct any electrical disturbance and we've kept his circulation going while we've tried but…we're not winning. I'm so sorry…'

Lisa bit her lip, staring down at the pile of discarded wrappers and the sharps bin where she'd been putting broken glass ampoules and needles from syringes. In a case like this, with a younger person involved, it had to be a unanimous team decision to stop the resuscitation. They had probably already gone for much longer than could have been deemed justified but nobody wanted to give up.

Nobody wanted to witness the distress of Carter's new wife a short time later when that decision was finally made. Peter took over caring for her while Tim and Hugh arranged for a stretcher to take him to the ship's morgue. Lisa and Janet cleaned up the mess of equipment and medical supplies and they took the trolley back to the medical centre to restock. It might be unthinkable but this kind of lightning could strike twice in the same place and they had to make sure that they were ready to respond.

'You okay?' Janet asked.

Lisa nodded. But the nod turned into a head shake. 'Not really,' she admitted. 'It's never nice to lose a patient but that was so sad. He was so young. And on his honeymoon...'

'I know.' Janet gave her a hug. 'The only good thing I can see is that he would have been so happy and it happened so suddenly he wouldn't have known anything about it. There are worse ways to go and things like that can happen at any age.'

Lisa nodded again. Her sister could have had a sudden death when she was only two.

'Is there someone you'd like to talk to? Hugh will be back soon. Or we could go and get a coffee.'

But Lisa was reaching into her pocket. 'It's okay,' she told Janet. 'But thanks. I promised I'd talk to my sister tonight and she'll understand.' Glancing at the screen, she saw that she'd missed a call from Abby hours ago now. Would she still be awake? Would it ruin her evening to know that Lisa was upset?

Abby rang straight back when Lisa texted so that she wouldn't disturb her if she was already asleep. It was a video call on her phone so that she could see that Abby was clearly not about to go to sleep either.

'Hey...' Lisa frowned at what she could see on her sister's face. 'What's up, Abby?'

Any thoughts of offloading onto her sister to receive the comfort and reassurance she needed evaporated instantly. Lisa might also be upset but it was Abby who burst into tears and struggled to get her words out.

'It's just... I've had...the most *awful* day.'

'Oh, no...' Lisa suddenly felt far too far away from the person she loved most in the world. All she wanted to do was hug her sister but all she could do was listen. 'Tell me what's happened...'

CHAPTER SIX

WAVE-WATCHING.

The river of churning water between the white waves on either side stretched as far as she could see into the night. How great would it be to be able to gather up any distressing thoughts and throw them overboard to get washed away and simply disappear into that endless sea?

It was an astonishingly therapeutic activity, Lisa decided, having wandered to the stern of the ship when she had finished her call to Abby. It had taken nearly an hour before Abby had started sounding anything like her normal determined and courageous self, but she'd had a real blow to her confidence today when she'd been taking a big step forward to achieving her dream of becoming a specialist hand therapist with her first clinical session.

'He thought I was there for therapy myself,' a still tearful Abby had told Lisa. *'And the look on his face when he found out I was there to treat him... Okay, maybe it might have been justified if I was there to help him learn to walk with a prosthetic leg or how to get down stairs with crutches but I was there to dress and splint his hand, Lise. Why do most people only see my wheelchair? Why can't they see* me?*'*

It was so unlike Abby to let something knock her like this but, as Lisa had reminded her, she had a lot going on in her life. She was adapting to living independently in a new environment, coping with an intensive regime of postgraduate study towards her new speciality and...the only family member she had might as well be on the other side of the world. When Abby had finished the call by telling Lisa how much she missed her, it had been Lisa who'd had tears rolling down her face—fortunately after she had ended the video call.

She needed to be home but she wasn't even halfway through this cruise and she couldn't walk out and leave the medical team short-handed, especially given that she was learning just how intense this job could be. There was a dead man somewhere on board this ship right now, and a grieving woman whose dream honeymoon had become her worst nightmare.

And she didn't really need to be home at all. She didn't need to do what she'd been doing her whole life and fret so much about Abby because she knew that her sister was going to be fine. Abby had already processed why the assumption had been made by her patient by the time she'd finished her conversation with Lisa. She'd forgiven the man for making it and had even laughed about it in the end, polishing up that armour that she'd built as a small child when she'd got stared or laughed at in the playground.

'I'll show them,' she'd say. *'I can do stuff too, even if my legs don't work.'*

Lisa lifted her gaze from the movement of the churning water so far below her and looked out to sea. They must be close to the Italian coastline now but she couldn't see it. All she could see was inky-black water below and an equally dark sky above with just the pinpricks of starlight. This massive ship suddenly seemed a tiny thing in the universe and, as a person standing there alone, Lisa felt totally insignificant.

And unbearably lonely. She wasn't as vital in Abby's life as she had been up till now and her own life suddenly seemed so much emptier, but she couldn't just turn away and take herself in a whole new direction either. She had to be very sure that Abby was safe and that meant staying close. Keeping herself safe.

'Hey...'

The voice behind her made her jump and then spin to see who was greeting her. Not that she needed to see. She'd known who it was as soon as she'd heard his voice.

'Hugh...what are you doing out here?' She was pathetically pleased to see him because it meant she wasn't alone any longer. And because they were friends. She needed a friend right now.

'Same as you, I expect,' Hugh said. 'Clearing my head. It's been quite a night, hasn't it?'

He looked exhausted, Lisa thought. He was still wearing his formal uniform but he had the sleeves of his white shirt rolled up and the neck undone, his jacket was hanging over one arm and she could see the tail of his tie that had been stuffed into a pocket of his black trousers. His hair was rumpled as well, as though he'd been combing it with his fingers. He looked more sombre than Lisa had ever seen him look, too, and that melted something in her heart.

She wanted to give him the hug that she hadn't been able to give Abby but, if she did that, she had the horrible feeling that she might burst into tears and how embarrassing would that be?

'Something like that doesn't happen that often,' Hugh said. 'And, when it does, it's usually someone in their eighties or nineties or with an underlying condition that means they're living on borrowed time. It's a lot harder to take when it's someone so much younger and apparently healthy, isn't it?'

Lisa nodded slowly, dropping her gaze so that Hugh wouldn't see her eyes fill with tears.

But he put a finger under her chin and she had to lift her face and there was no hiding how she was feeling. Hugh's gaze was searching. It seemed as if he was absorbing everything she was feeling. That he wanted to understand because then he might be able to fix something and the impression that he cared enough to do that was almost enough to undo Lisa completely in that moment.

'Come with me,' was all he said, dropping his arm around her shoulders. 'Peter and Tim are covering the rest of the night and I have something to show you.'

Lisa was aware of the weight of Hugh's arm and that her feet were already moving in response to his encouragement. She had no idea what it was he wanted to show her, but the last time she had gone somewhere with him he'd promised that she wouldn't regret it and he'd given her a memory that she would treasure for ever. It wasn't hard to trust him now.

'We did everything we possibly could, you know,' Hugh told her when they were alone in the elevator, going down to a lower deck. 'And you were an important part of that, getting the defibrillator on scene so fast. Even if he'd been in the best-equipped emergency department on land he wouldn't have survived. I'm guessing he had a catastrophic heart attack or a serious, undiagnosed cardiomyopathy.'

'He was on his honeymoon,' Lisa said. 'How sad is that?' She walked ahead of Hugh as the elevator doors opened. 'It should have been the happiest time of his life.'

The huff of sound from Hugh made Lisa turn swiftly and his eyebrows rose at the look she was giving him.

'Sorry… It's not funny at all. It's just that… well, the first time I ever came on a cruise ship, I was on my honeymoon.'

Lisa could feel her jaw dropping. 'You're *married*?' Oddly, there seemed to be a sink-ing sensation in her stomach at the same time. Because she was disappointed that a married man would be playing around with so many other women, perhaps?

But Hugh was shaking his head emphatically. 'Nope. Never been married. Never intend to be either. One honeymoon was enough and I did it solo.' His mouth tilted on one side. 'Apart from everyone I met along the way, of course, but I did it without a wife.'

'What happened?' The personal question popped out before Lisa could stop it but, as a distraction from her own less than happy thoughts, this was irresistible.

Hugh shrugged. 'I'd gone to my best friend's house a couple of days before the wedding to deliver his suit because he was going to be my best man. That was when I found him in bed with my fiancée, Catherine. It was a no-brainer to cancel the wedding but I couldn't cancel the cruise and I thought, seeing as I'd paid for it all and arranged time off work, I might as well get away for a couple of weeks.'

'So this was before you started working on ships?'

'It was *why* I started working on ships.'

Lisa was so fascinated by this story she simply walked through the door that Hugh had opened but then she stopped and stared.

'This is someone's cabin,' she said.

'It is indeed,' Hugh agreed. 'It's my cabin.'

It was a lot bigger than Lisa's cabin. There was a desk with its surface crowded by a laptop computer, scattered medical journals and a collection of empty mugs. The chair in front of it had Hugh's normal white uniform draped over it. There was a couch and armchairs in front of doors that led out to a generous balcony, a door that obviously led to a bathroom and a double bed that looked rumpled enough to give the impression that Hugh had just climbed out of it.

Lisa's gaze slid sideways, trying to imagine him in pyjamas. Nope... If ever there was a man who would sleep naked, surely it would be Hugh Patterson. The uninvited thought was enough to make her close her eyes for a moment as she willed her cheeks not to start glowing like Rudolph the reindeer's nose.

'Um…' She cleared her throat. 'What was it you were saying?'

Lisa looked about as uncomfortable as she had the first time Hugh had ever seen her, first on the wharf in Barcelona when they both knew she'd been watching him kiss Carlotta and then when he'd met her in the medical centre and she'd known she would be working with him for the next couple of weeks.

But, until she realised he had brought her into his private, personal space, he'd been doing a good job of distracting her from the misery that he assumed was due to their unsuccessful resuscitation efforts this evening. He hadn't seen her with tears in her eyes like that before and he suspected it would take something huge to make Lisa Phillips cry so it had induced an odd squeezing sensation in his chest that meant he had to try and fix things.

'Ah…' Hugh decided to ignore her embarrassment and act like it was no big deal that his cabin was messy and he hadn't even made his bed properly. He walked towards the sitting room corner to open the balcony doors. That way, Lisa wouldn't feel like she was trapped and it was a nice enough evening to sit out there if that helped. 'I was saying that my solo honeymoon was the reason I took a job as a ship's doctor. I had been about to take up a position in a general practice in the nice outer London suburb I'd grown up in. I was all set to settle down and move back into the family home and raise my two point four children—you know, the whole nine yards.'

Lisa was shaking her head. 'You were really in love, weren't you? It must have been absolutely devastating.'

'Better to happen then than when those two and a bit kids were involved.' Hugh kept his tone light. He also needed to change the subject because, like his privileged background, it was something he preferred not to talk about. To anyone. He *had* been devastated. He'd gone on board his first cruise ship feeling totally betrayed and crushed and, for some weird reason, he almost felt like telling Lisa every gruesome detail. Because he knew she would understand? That she would care?

'Anyway...there was an incident on board. Or rather on shore. One of the passengers was riding a donkey on a Greek island and he fell off and dislocated his shoulder. I managed to get it relocated for him and used his clothes to splint it in place, got him back to the ship and then ended up helping to X-ray him to make sure it was all okay.'

Lisa had followed him towards the balcony but now she sat down on the edge of the couch as she listened to his story.

'The doctor I was working with told me they were looking for new medical staff and it all came together. I didn't have to settle in one place or start thinking about real estate or nursery schools. I didn't need to get bored by turning up to the same place every day to do the same job. I could live and work like I was on a permanent holiday and get an endless variety of medical challenges, some of them as big as anything you'd get on land—like tonight.'

Hugh turned away, towards the small fridge tucked behind one of the armchairs. That had been more than two years ago now. It didn't feel so much like a permanent holiday any longer. He was, in fact, turning up to the same place every day to do the same job, wasn't he? And, yes, he was living the dream with all the fabulous places he got to visit and the glamour of being a ship's officer but…sometimes it all felt a bit transitory, with nothing solid to hang onto. Even friends that you made along the way—like Lisa—didn't necessarily stay in your life.

This living the dream felt pretty darned lonely sometimes, in fact…

Empty, even?

'Right.' He opened the fridge. 'This is what I wanted to show you.'

'You're kidding.' Lisa looked shocked. 'Champagne? Tonight—after how *awful* it's been?'

Her voice wobbled a little on the last few words and Hugh felt that squeeze in his chest again. He opened the freezer compartment of the fridge to pick out the frosty glasses that lived there and then went to sit beside Lisa, putting the glasses on the coffee table in front of her.

'Have you heard of Napoleon Bonaparte?' he asked casually.

'Of course. I loved history at school.' Lisa looked surprised at the random question but there was a hint of a smile on her face as she played along. 'Short guy, born in Corsica, married Josephine and crowned himself emperor of France. He was famous for saying that an army marches on its stomach, I believe.'

Hugh nodded. He was removing the foil and twisting the wire around the cork on the bottle. 'He had something to say about champagne, too.'

'Oh?'

'Yep. He said that in victory you deserve champagne but in defeat you *need* it.' As if to applaud the statement, the cork shot towards the ceiling with a satisfyingly loud popping sound. The sound of Lisa's laughter was even more satisfying.

'You're incorrigible, Hugh, you know that?'

'I'd agree if I knew what that meant.' Hugh suppressed a smile as he filled a glass to hand to Lisa. 'But it's a good thing, yes?' He touched his glass to hers. *'Santé,'* he murmured.

'You know perfectly well what it means.' But there was genuine amusement in her eyes before she closed them as she took an appreciative sip of her sparkling wine.

'It's just as good as the first time,' she said. 'Maybe even better. That doesn't often happen, does it?'

'Some things actually get better the more often you do them,' he said, 'And some things you never want to do for a second time. Once burnt, forever shy.'

'Mmm...'

He could feel Lisa's gaze on him and, as soon as he turned towards her, he knew she was thinking about the spectacular crash and burn of his wedding plans. He could feel the moment her thoughts changed from sympathy to something else, though. She was thinking about the kinds of things he had done often enough to become expert in. Like kissing... Any second now, she was going to go back to that assumption she'd made that he fell into bed with every willing woman who tried to attract his attention.

He held her gaze steadily, making a silent statement that she was completely wrong in that assumption. That there were actually very few women he had fallen—or wanted to fall—into bed with.

But... He didn't need that spear of sensation in his body to confirm what he suddenly realised. Lisa Phillips was definitely one of those women and, at this moment in time, it felt like she was the only one.

Stunned by the realisation, Hugh put his glass carefully down on the table as an excuse to break the eye contact but he was a fraction of a second too late. He'd seen the way her pupils were dilating. She not only knew what he was thinking, she was responding to it.

Hugh pulled in a slow breath but he wasn't about to shake off the detour his brain, and his body, were determined to take. He wanted her. He wanted to see that flicker of desire in her eyes get kindled into a flame. Maybe he wanted to tease her in a completely different way from any he would have considered before now—to create enough frustration to be able to make getting tipped into paradise all the more intense. Would the expression in her eyes be anything like the first time she had tasted real champagne?

Would he be making a terrible mistake if he tried to find out? Just proving that Lisa's assumptions about his lifestyle were not wrong? Or was he right in suspecting that she might want this as much as he did?

He turned back to meet her gaze again, knowing that she would see that last question in his eyes. Maybe he didn't really have a choice here, given the way his desire was exploding now that it had been acknowledged. But Lisa did have a choice and he would totally respect that. A cold shower might well be in the cards in his very near future.

* * *

Oh...*my*... That *look*...

Lisa had to swallow her mouthful of champagne in a hurry. Nobody had ever looked at her like that. Ever. As if she was the most desirable thing in the entire world. As if he wanted to do a whole lot more than simply kiss her. And every single cell in Lisa's body was not only reminding her of what it was like to be kissed by this man but making a plea to find out what doing more than kissing would be like.

This was, she realised, the first time in her life that she actually, desperately wanted to get really intimate with someone. Oh, she'd had the usual teenage curiosity about sex but that had been mixed with doubt that the experience might not live up to expectations that had been set by some of the books she'd read and she'd been so right. Early attempts had been fumbling and embarrassing. With her more recent choices of boyfriends it had been a lot better. Enjoyable, even, but still nothing like having fireworks going off or the earth spinning on its axis or a herd of unicorns galloping off into the sunset.

She had, with the help of one of those boy-friends, come to the conclusion that the fault lay completely on her side, and in a way that had been a relief because perhaps there was a part of her that had decided long ago that she really didn't deserve that kind of plea-sure. Whatever the cause, Lisa had given up believing in any of that hype about how good sex could be—as far as she was con-cerned, anyway.

Until Hugh Patterson had kissed her the other night, that was…

Lisa could imagine that she was standing on the edge of a precipice here. She could— and undoubtedly *should*—step back onto firm, safe ground. If she let herself fall, there were two possibilities. One was that Hugh would catch her—probably with his lips to start with—and the other was that she would just keep falling, in which case she might crash into an embarrassing heap because he would find out that she wasn't very good at sex, but…

But… There was something about tonight that felt different. Hugh had found her at one of the lowest points she could remember in a very long time. She was missing Abby and worried about her but aware that her sister would actually be able to cope perfectly well without her, which made this a turning point in her life, but it was scary because she couldn't imagine such a different future. She had been gutted by the death of their patient. She'd realised what an insignificant speck she was in the face of a limitless night sky and sea and she'd been feeling *so* lonely.

His company had been a godsend because it was exactly what she needed to counteract that loneliness. The way he'd held her face up with his finger under her chin and tried to read her face like a book had made her feel as if her well-being was important to him. That he was really seeing her. He didn't know a lot about her life, other than how important her sister was to her, but it felt like he knew more than any man ever had.

He'd shared something personal, too. Physically, as in bringing her into his private cabin, but emotionally as well, by telling her the story of how he'd been betrayed by the woman he'd loved enough to be about to marry. Above all, he'd made her laugh. He'd given her a moment that had obliterated the worry for Abby, fear for the future and the grief for the man who'd died tonight.

Right now, he was silently asking her if she wanted to be made love to and the answer was a cry that came from somewhere very deep in Lisa's soul. She felt astonishingly vulnerable in this moment but…she trusted this man and she'd never before wanted so much to be as close to another person as possible. She needed that comfort. To escape for a little while from any worries or sadness in her world. To know that she wasn't as insignificant as she'd imagined?

She still hesitated, however. Because, judging by that kiss, Hugh was an expert in all things sexual and she…well, he was going to be disappointed, wasn't he?

Oddly, the nerves in her fingers seemed to have stopped working because she made no attempt to hang onto her glass when Hugh

gently took it from her and put it down beside his on the table. The nerves in her lips,
on the other hand, were in overdrive as he
slowly turned back, cupped her chin in one
hand and touched her lips with his own in
the same way he had the first time he'd done
this. Such a feather-light touch, a soft rub, a
tiny lick. Infinitely subtle changes of pressure as if her mouth was being not only invited to dance but being led around a dance
floor so that being good at it was effortless.
A tiny sound escaped her lips as Lisa let
herself sink blissfully deeper into that kiss.

It was that tiny sound that totally undid
Hugh.

That took him to a place he didn't recognise, in fact. He'd seen the heart-break-
ing vulnerability in Lisa's eyes before he'd
kissed her and that had set off alarm bells
like never before because he knew he was
in a position to hurt Lisa. But she knew as
well as he did that this was only about tonight and he could feel that her need was
as urgent as his own. And…what really did

something unprecedented to his head—and his heart—was that he could see the trust she was gifting him.

That sound was like the sigh of someone who'd pushed past a final barrier and could see the place they were desperate to get to. And, even more than how much his own body was craving the release of indulging this astonishingly powerful desire, that sound made Hugh want this to be something special for Lisa. She might not be a virgin but there was something that told him Lisa was nervous of sex for some reason. Afraid of it, even? He had given her the joy of her first taste of real champagne. Maybe, if he took things slowly and gently, he could give her the knowledge that sex could be just as good. Perhaps even better...

So that's what he did. He lost track of time but it didn't matter a damn how long this took. He took his sweet time getting them both naked and into his bed and then introducing himself to every inch of Lisa's body with his hands and his lips. He could feel every time she got tense or tried to please *him* by hurrying things along so he would slow her hands. Capture them and hold them above her head for a moment or two.

'Shh… It's all good,' he would murmur to reassure her, before kissing her for as long as it took for her to relax again. 'Wait… We've got all the time in the world.'

Maybe it was the gentle motion of the sea way beneath them.

Or maybe a taste of champagne on top of the emotional and physical fatigue of this evening had put Lisa into a space like no other.

Or—and this was far the most likely—it was because this was Hugh she was with. A man who clearly knew his way around a woman's body. It seemed like he knew *her* body better than she knew it herself. And whenever she had the fear that he was going to discover that she was being a complete fraud and only pretending that she was loving this, he would simply back off. Slow the pace and force her to be patient when all she wanted to try and do was give him the pleasure of the release he more than deserved.

She'd try again in just a minute, she decided. Surely he'd had enough of trying to bring her to a climax. It wasn't going to happen and the worry was that he would guess that she was faking it, like others had, unless she could be more convincing than she had ever been before. But the flicker of doubt came and went, along with the determination to move and touch Hugh again in a way she was sure he wouldn't be able to resist. She was caught, she realised, in an escalating tension being created by the movement of Hugh's fingers.

She put her hand over his to ask him to stop but he ignored her and, in alarm, Lisa opened her eyes, only to find that Hugh's face was right beside her own and he was watching her. And that was when it happened. She was falling. Falling into wave after wave of the most intense pleasure she'd ever experienced in her life.

Her astonished gasp triggered what she'd been trying to achieve for what felt like for ever to make sure that this was good for Hugh and, even as those extraordinary waves began to recede, she heard his groan of need and then she could feel him inside her and, unbelievably, the new movement was building that tension all over again.

This time, when she unravelled, he was holding her tightly in his arms so she could feel the shudders in his body and knew that they were both falling. He was still holding her as she tried to slow her breathing afterwards, aware of the pounding of both their hearts. Aware that Hugh was watching her again and there was a question in his eyes but a smile on his face as if he already knew the answer.

'Good?' he whispered.

Lisa could feel a smile curving her own lips. 'Unicorns,' she whispered back.

The sparkle of delight in Hugh's eyes and the way his smile widened told Lisa that he understood. That he couldn't be happier that she'd found it magic and the knowledge that he was so happy that she was happy gave Lisa a whole new sensation of falling.

Falling in love?

'So, what do you reckon?' Hugh was still smiling. 'Is sex as good as or better than champagne?'

That's what this had been, Lisa reminded herself hurriedly. Just sex. One of those "good things" in life—like dancing or fine wine. It might have been the best sex she'd ever had in her life but she and Hugh weren't lovers, they were only friends. But that didn't seem to matter right now because Lisa was still under the spell of the magic and it seemed that she was stepping into a whole new world.

'I'm not sure,' she murmured. 'I might have to test that theory again sometime.'

The growling sound that Hugh made was most definitely one of approval. 'I think that's very wise. One should never jump to conclusions about important things. I'm happy to help with the research.'

But Lisa wriggled free as he began to trail kisses down her neck and onto her shoulder. Her world had just been rocked in a rather spectacular manner but reality was making its presence felt and there was suddenly a

beat of fear to be found in the knowledge
that she had lost control to such an extent.
That, for heaven knows how long, the most
important thing in her life had been Hugh
and what was happening between them.
She'd never let desire overwhelm her like
that before. It was dangerous because it distracted you and, if you let important things
slip from your grasp when you were distracted, it could ruin your life. That she
could remember a lifelong mantra she had
just ignored but still feel so incredibly happy
was confusing, to say the least.

'I need to go,' she said. 'I think it's time
I got back to my own cabin and got some
sleep.'

Hugh let her slip out of his grasp. 'No
problem,' he responded. 'We've got all the
time in the world for that research.'

Which wasn't true, Lisa thought as she
moved quietly along deserted narrow hall-
ways a few minutes later. They had little
more than another week before the fantasy
of shipboard life, exotic locations and now
mind-blowing sex would have to come to

an end. But that didn't seem to matter either. Because, even if tonight was the only night she could ever have with Hugh Patterson, it had been worth it. She wasn't broken after all. She'd just needed a person who cared enough to show her that and, while she couldn't possibly be *in* love with someone like Hugh, she could love him for giving her that. For making her feel that perhaps she *did* deserve that kind of joy in her life.

And, even if it was dangerous to be distracted like that, it had nothing to do with her real life, did it? Abby was safe. Lisa was here, earning extra money to make sure she could maintain that safety for both of them. So the distraction was confined. And limited. It could only last a matter of days, until this cruise was finished and she flew back to her real life. A handful of days was just a blip in anyone's lifetime.

Could there be any real harm in enjoying it while it lasted?

CHAPTER SEVEN

SO...SEX WAS one of the things that got better the more often you did it.

Or, she should qualify that, Lisa realised, because it was only sex with Hugh that continued to surprise and delight her on new levels every time. The total opposite to her past experience in relationships, in fact, when sex had become progressively more predictable and dull. Anxiety inducing as well, because she'd known she wasn't performing as well as expected.

She knew why it was so different, of course. Hugh was the complete opposite to anyone she had ever chosen to get close to in the past. The bad boy versus the sensible, safe kind of man. Not that they were in a relationship. They both knew that this was never going to be any more than a friendship and that their time together was limited. Perhaps that was why they were both making the most of it.

Keeping it secret was part of the thrill as well. Maybe that was making it safer to enjoy because it confirmed that this was a friendship with hidden benefits rather than a relationship that carried responsibilities. Or perhaps it really was frowned upon for crew members to hook up, but whatever the reason was, the agreement was tacit and became more enjoyable as the days ticked past. There were a couple of long days at sea as the ship sailed around the bottom of Italy to the Greek Islands on the itinerary and then back again.

They both became very good at the game of working together without betraying how close they were, resisting the urge to hold eye contact a little too long, or engineer moments when their hands or bodies might touch as they moved in sometimes confined spaces. They were being careful not to be seen visiting each other's cabins and spending only a part of each night together, and they could make it appear that they went on shore leave separately but meeting up as soon as they were out of sight.

Like they had for a delightful day on the island of Mykonos, where they had met up at a private beach that was not on the usual tourist radar. There were small fishing boats in the nearby port, pelicans that seemed to be expert in posing for photographs and a waveless beach that was like the biggest swimming pool ever.

And like they had again today as they'd reached the second-last destination of this cruise and it was Blue Watch's turn to have shore leave, having stayed on the ship for the visit to Santorini.

With the cruise ship docked in the port of Salerno as they reached Italy again on the way back to Spain, there had been multiple choices for a day's outing. There were buses going to Naples, to Sorrento with a boat trip to the island of Capri, and a tour that took in both Mount Vesuvius and the ancient city of Pompeii.

They were all destinations that took Lisa's

breath away so why did she avoid every one of them?

Because Hugh had offered her something far more enticing. Another day alone with him and somewhere that no one else would be likely to be going.

'I know this walk,' he told her. 'It's called The Valley of the Ancient Mills. And it's right under everybody's noses but they'll be jumping on the buses to go further afield. This valley is quiet and green, and full of the ruins of old mills and a river and waterfalls, and we can walk up the hills towards a gorgeous village called Ravello, but on the way is another little village. I don't even know the name of it but it has a restaurant with a terrace and a view and—'

'Stop…' Lisa pressed her finger against Hugh's lips. 'I'm sold. How could I go past a restaurant with a terrace?'

She couldn't. Not after the most romantic evening ever, in that French restaurant, even though there had been nothing romantic happening between them yet. How much more fabulous would it be to have a setting like that when you were with your lover? Well, okay, she couldn't—and didn't—think of Hugh as her lover and she knew there was a definite limit to this fling and that this outing today would be almost the last, but she was making memories here, wasn't she? And memories could be woven into a fantasy that she could enjoy for ever. A private fantasy. She hadn't confessed the new development in her life to Abby, although her sister had guessed something was going on.

'You just look so...different, Lise. So... happy. I've never seen you kind of glowing like this before.'

'I'm happy you're okay. That that last clinical session was the total opposite of that horrible first one. She won't be the first patient to see you as an inspiration.'

But Abby hadn't been convinced. *'It's more than that. You look like, I don't know, a kid on Christmas morning.'*

'I'm loving this cruise, that's all. I could go to Pompeii on our next stop, if I want. Or walk up to the top of Mount Vesuvius. How incredible is that?'

She had convinced Abby that her excitement was at the prospect of seeing such famous sights but the real reason was far simpler.

'Actually, you had me at the name of the valley,' she told Hugh. 'It sounds very... romantic.'

And it was. It was as green and quiet as Hugh had promised and the shade was welcome in the increasing heat of a late Italian morning. There were wild cyclamen making a carpet of pale pink beneath the trees, the buzzing of bees and bird calls nearby and the refreshing ripple of the river not far away. There were moss-covered ruins of the old stone mills and, best of all, they had this track all to themselves. A private world. Hugh took Lisa's hand to help her up a rocky part of the path but he didn't let go when she was back on smooth ground.

Instead, he pulled her close and kissed her with one of those slow and, oh, so thorough kisses that Lisa was quite probably getting addicted to because they were a drug all by themselves. She could feel herself floating away within seconds towards that place where nothing else existed. Just herself and Hugh and the promise of absolute bliss…

But Hugh broke the kiss too soon this time, albeit reluctantly.

'We need to keep going,' he said. 'We've got a bit further to go and this weather's not going to last.'

'I heard that there was stormy weather coming but I thought it was a few days away yet.'

'The big storms probably won't catch us until we're somewhere between Sardinia and Malaga on our way home but it's going to get overcast later today and will probably rain by tomorrow.'

Lisa didn't want to think about arriving in Malaga, which was when she would be leaving the ship to fly back to England. 'I hope the sun lasts while we have lunch on that terrace,' she said. 'I can't wait.'

'I hope it lasts a bit longer. If we've got time and enough energy, we can walk further up to Ravello and go exploring and then get a taxi or bus back to the ship. There's an amazing old villa in Ravello called the Villa Rufolo and it's well worth visiting.'

'You know so many places to go.'

'I've done it so many times. Too many, perhaps. I usually try to find something new to see at every destination but...' he smiled at Lisa. 'It's actually a lot more fun sharing the things I already know with you because... I don't know...it makes them more special.'

His words made Lisa feel special. In fact, knowing that Hugh was getting genuine pleasure from sharing things that he liked with her was giving her an even stronger connection to this man who had the most gorgeous smile in the world. It gave her a bit of lump in her throat, to be honest.

They finally left the beautiful valley and its mills behind and followed a path that gave them wonderful views past forests and lemon groves and terraced fields of tomatoes to where the town of Amalfi nestled right beside the sparkling blue of the Mediterranean. The path led through stone archways that were charmingly decorated with old wicker baskets and unusual-looking utensils.

By the time they reached the restaurant, they were ready to rest and enjoy a meal. They both ordered an *insalata caprese*—a salad of delicious slices of fresh local tomatoes, mozzarella cheese and basil leaves that was drizzled with olive oil. It came with a basket of fresh, crusty bread and was the most perfect-looking lunch Lisa had ever seen. She had to take a photo of it for Abby.

Hugh ordered Prosecco as well.

'Think of it as Italian champagne,' he told Lisa, with a wink. *'Saluti, cara.'*

Cara. Didn't that mean something like *darling* or *sweetheart*? Lisa touched her glass to Hugh's and met his gaze over the top of the glasses. The warmth in those brown eyes and the echoes of the endearment he had just used stole her breath away and it was at that moment that Lisa realised she was in trouble.

She had known right from the start that this was temporary. That it was just a shipboard fling that was going to end very soon and it was highly unlikely that she would ever see Hugh Patterson again. But she also knew that it was not going to be easy. At this moment, if felt as if it could very well be devastating.

Because she'd fallen in love with him. It had probably happened, without her even realising, that night when he'd managed to make her laugh when she'd been feeling so awful. When he'd taken her to his bed and changed her life for ever. When she'd mistakenly analysed her feelings as lust rather than love, but this was so much deeper than anything purely sexual. Lisa wanted the closeness and connection they'd discovered to last for ever. She wanted, in particular, to freeze this moment in time when it felt like she could fall into that gaze and never want to come up for air.

Maybe it was an omen that a shadow noticeably darkened this idyllic scene as a first bank of clouds drifted overhead to obscure the sun. It was Hugh who broke that eye contact to look up at the sky.

'Uh-oh,' he murmured. 'Maybe that storm's on its way a bit quicker than they predicted.'

'Mmm.' But Lisa wasn't thinking about bad weather as she made a concerned sound and even suppressed a shiver. She was thinking of something that was going to be a lot less pleasant to endure.

Saying goodbye to Hugh…

Had Hugh really thought that Lisa Phillips was uptight and controlling?

That she wouldn't trust anyone else enough to even help her carry her suitcase?

That she was the complete opposite of the type of women he could ever be attracted to?

Oh, man…how wrong could a person be?

As if she'd picked up on his thought by telepathy, Lisa turned from the window of the bus to catch his gaze. There was awe in those amazing eyes, thanks to the view down the mountainside to the town of Amalfi they were heading back to, but there was also a bit of fear at the speed at which the bus driver was taking these hairpin bends on the narrow road.

'I guess he knows what he's doing,' she

muttered. 'He must have done it plenty of times before.'

That was so like Lisa, wasn't it? She might be afraid to some degree and she might be determined to excel in everything she did but she was still prepared to trust someone else, which gave her a very endearing, almost childlike quality.

She trusted *him* now. On a very different level from anything he would have imagined them sharing.

He had wanted a certain level of trust from Lisa as soon as he'd realised they were going to be spending a lot of time together for a couple of weeks. He'd wanted to tease her and make her a little less 'uptight'. He'd wanted to show her that there were things in life that were meant to be enjoyed and she was missing out on most of them.

What he hadn't realised was that sharing those things with her would make them so different for him. He'd been drinking champagne and having sex with beautiful women, travelling to amazing places and just getting the most out of his life for a very long time now, but doing exactly the same things with Lisa was like doing them himself for the very first time because they felt *that* different.

The bus was leaning as it took another bend and Hugh could feel the pit of his own stomach dropping as he looked over Lisa's shoulder to the drop below the side of the road. The bus seemed to be clinging to the road by the edge of its tyres but Lisa's squeak of terror was half excitement and the way her fingers clutched his arm so dramatically made him smile.

Maybe this was what it was like when you had a child, he thought, and you got to see the world all over again from their perspective. You could experience the sourness of a lemon perhaps as you laughed at the face they made. Or the joy of feeling your body fly through the air that was enough to make you shriek with glee when someone pushed you on a swing for the first time. Perhaps what made this so different with Lisa was that it was an adult version of rediscovery.

The sex had been a revelation every single

time. So familiar but so new as well—as if everything had suddenly become colour instead of just black and white. The joy on her face today, when she'd had to stop and simply gaze at the beauty of that walk past the ancient paper mills, and her eyes closing in bliss when she'd had her first mouthful of that mix of tomatoes and cheese and basil...

Hugh had never tasted a salad that good himself and yet he'd eaten an *insalata caprese* countless times before. It wasn't that those astonishingly bright red local tomatoes had that much more flavour. Or that the olive oil was especially good. Hugh knew that it was being with Lisa that was making things so different and that was more than a little disturbing.

Because it was true that she wasn't his "type" at all. That when he had first met her, when he had actually been with the sophisticated Carlotta—who was exactly his type—he wouldn't have dreamed of asking Lisa out. The notion that he might be able to make love to her time and time again and feel like he could never get enough of her would have been a joke. If he'd had a premonition that doing something as ordinary as sightseeing with her could be so delightful he would have known he needed to stay well clear. He had invented what he thought of as his type because those women were safe. They didn't want loyalty or commitment or to risk betrayal any more than he did.

It had been too long, hadn't it? He'd become complacent and hadn't realised that it was even possible for anyone to get past his protective barriers. He'd considered himself to be completely safe from feeling like this again. That *pride* in being the one to provide something that gave joy to someone else. That desire that had nothing to do with sex but was a wish to keep providing things like that. To protect someone and cherish them.

That was what falling in love was all about, wasn't it?

He'd started out seeing Lisa as someone who could be the little sister he'd never had. How could this determined but naïve, petite, shaggy red-haired woman with unusual eyes and freckles to match their hazel brown have become the most beautiful person Hugh had ever known? He'd been in love once before but how he was starting to feel about Lisa had the potential to blow that past love out of the water and make it barely worth re-membering.

That was a little terrifying, he had to admit.

Except that Lisa was nothing like Cath-erine, his ex-fiancée, was she? This was someone who had actually sacrificed prob-ably more than she was letting on in order to care for someone she loved—her sister Abby. Lisa would have that kind of loyalty to anyone she loved, if she ever let some-one in to that degree, and she wouldn't lie about how she felt either. Or, if she tried, he would be able to see immediately that she wasn't being truthful because he could read her face like a book now thanks to watching it so carefully in her unguarded moments.

And that meant he could trust Lisa. On a level that he'd never thought he would ever trust a woman again. But what, if anything, should he do about that? There was a clock ticking here. In a matter of only a couple of days this woman was going to walk out of his life and back to her own. If he didn't want that to happen he would have to make some big decisions in a hurry. But not yet... He might recognise that he was feeling the way you did when you fell in love but that didn't mean it had actually happened yet, did it? Or that Lisa even felt the same way.

They were nearly back at sea level now, passing the first houses of Amalfi, and they'd need to hurry to get a taxi back to Salerno and back on board the ship in good time before they left the port. There would be no time for a while to give such a serious matter the amount of thought it needed and Hugh could feel himself releasing his breath in a sigh of relief as they climbed down the steps of the bus. He could just stop thinking about it and enjoy the present for a bit longer. He'd lived this way for long enough to know that it could work.

The smile on Lisa's face as she skipped a step to catch up with his long stride was enough to make it well worth thinking only about the next few hours. Getting back on board, an evening surgery, dinner and then… Hugh held Lisa's gaze for a long moment as he sent a silent invitation for her to come to his cabin later tonight. The way her smile faded as the colour in her eyes changed from golden brown to something more molten was enough to let him know that the invitation had been received and accepted.

He couldn't bring himself to break that gaze. He opened his mouth and he knew that the words that were about to come out would change everything.

Three little words.

I love you…

They were there. In his head. On the tip of his tongue. But something stopped him. Maybe it was the tiny frown line that appeared between Lisa's eyes when she heard a sound from her phone. She dived into her bag to find it.

'That's Abby texting me. She was going back to the house to check things for me today. I hope everything's all right.'

Hugh could sense that Lisa's attention was

a very long way away from him now. She
was back in her real life for the moment.
Away from her working holiday fling. In a
place he would never belong.

'Everything okay?'

'She's stressing because she's found a pile
of mail behind the door and she's wants to
know if she should open it. I've told her to
leave it where it is. I'll deal with it all when
I get home.'

Her glance was apologetic, as if she understood that her real life had nothing to
do with him. Or that she didn't want it to
have anything to do with him? Hugh took
a deeper breath and he could feel his mind
clearing noticeably. He was certainly going
to miss Lisa when she left the ship in Malaga
but he could cope if he had to and that would
be a lot easier than grappling with concepts
he had given up even thinking about a very
long time ago. Things like settling down to a
more ordinary job somewhere. Getting married. Having a family.

Good grief... Hugh turned away from Lisa
and hurriedly raised his arm to flag down a

taxi. Had the thought of getting *married* actually entered his head in that flash of muddled thoughts? The sooner they were back on board his beloved ship and in his familiar environment the better. He had to put a stop to this before he did something really crazy.

Like asking Lisa to marry him...

Something had changed but, for the life of her, Lisa couldn't put her finger on quite what it could be.

They'd had such a lovely day together with that walk up through the valley and the delicious lunch and then exploring the mountain town and that crazy bus ride back to the coast. She was quite sure that Hugh had enjoyed the day as much as she had but he seemed a little edgy when they opened the medical centre for the evening surgery. Was it because the wind had picked up as the ship had eased out into more open sea? Lisa could feel the gentle roll of bigger swells beneath them, although she wasn't finding it alarming at all.

'Is it likely to be a problem, getting a storm while we're at sea?'

'Hard to say. Sometimes the captain can navigate around the bad weather and modern ships have stabilisers that help a lot, although it's surprising to a lot of people how rough the Mediterranean can get. Usually they just blow past with nothing more than a lot of people getting very seasick or complaining that some decks and the swimming pools are closed. Thanks for the reminder. I'd better check our supplies of anti-motion-sickness medications.'

'What do you use?' Lisa followed him into the pharmacy room.

'We give out the usual over-the-counter remedies to anyone who asks and they're also available in many of the shops if there gets to be too much of a queue here. The shops also have things like different forms of ginger and peppermint, which we often advise people to try. Other advice includes eating something, like dry crackers, getting some fresh air on the balcony or deck or going to the centre of the ship where it's more stable.'

'And if it's serious?'

'We've got good stocks of promethazine and metoclopramide.' Hugh shut and locked the glass-fronted cupboard he'd opened. 'And plenty of saline if someone gets really dehydrated. Here...' He scooped a lot of small packages out of a drawer to hand to Lisa. 'Let's keep these supplies of Dramamine at the front desk. If they're mild cases you can dispense this and send them home when you're triaging.' He glanced over his shoulder as he led the way out of the pharmacy. 'You're not worried about this storm, are you?'

'Um...no...' But Lisa bit her lip. 'I did find some videos online, though, that looked a bit scary. Restaurants with all the tables and even a piano rolling one way and then the other and taking people out on the way.'

Hugh was smiling. 'Have you seen that movie with the ship and the iceberg? That's a good one, too. It's just as well that we don't get many icebergs in the Mediterranean.'

Lisa loved that smile so much. She loved the way there were crinkles of amusement on either side of those gorgeous brown eyes but, most of all, she loved that he was checking how she was feeling about something and was trying to make her laugh to ease any worry. She *did* laugh and, suddenly, whatever tension had been in the air this evening evaporated, along with any nerves about stormy weather. She was with Hugh. They could handle whatever came their way.

Including a patient she was worried about the moment she walked into the medical centre and had to snatch a breath even while she was introducing herself.

'You're sounding very wheezy, Michelle. Are you asthmatic?'

The young woman nodded. 'It's not getting better...so I thought... I'd come in...'

'Good thinking. Come with me.' Lisa led her straight to the treatment room. 'I'm just going to check your blood pressure and heart rate and the oxygen level in your blood.' She put the clip on his finger. 'Have you been using your inhaler?'

'Yes…lots…'

She got Michelle to blow into a peak flow meter as well.

'What do you normally blow?'

'On a good day…four hundred.'

She was down to a lot less than three hundred now.

'I'm sure the doctor will want to start a nebuliser at least. Let's give you another pillow or two to keep you a bit more upright and I'll go and find him.'

Hugh was with another patient who had run out of his high blood pressure medication a week ago but had thought it wouldn't matter until he'd started getting bad headaches, but one look at Lisa's face and he stood up.

'Wait there, Jim,' he told his patient. 'I'll be back very soon. We're going to admit you to our little hospital here for a while so we can keep an eye on you while you have some intravenous medication to bring your blood pressure down in a controlled manner.'

Jim's wife had come to the appointment with him. 'I told you it was serious,' she growled. 'Don't you dare move. I'm going back to the cabin to get your pyjamas and toothbrush. You're going to stay here until the doctor says you're okay.'

Hugh was right beside Lisa as she sped back to the treatment room. 'I'm worried that her asthma isn't responding to her inhaler. She's not speaking more than three to four words per breath and her oxygen saturation is down to ninety-six percent. Respiration rate is twenty-five, heart rate is one twenty, and peak flow is not much more than fifty percent of normal for her. Do you want me to set up a nebuliser?'

'Absolutely. We might need to start some IV corticosteroids as well. And get an arterial blood gas measurement.'

By the time Hugh had listened to Michelle's chest, Lisa had a nebuliser mask ready, with medication in the chamber and oxygen running through at a high enough rate to produce a good vapour. She slipped the elastic over the back of Michelle's head and rearranged her pillows to make it more comfortable for her to sit upright.

She worked with Hugh to find and hand him everything he needed to set up an IV line and then the more difficult procedure of inserting a cannula into an artery in Michelle's wrist so that they would be able to get a far more accurate indication of how much circulating oxygen she had in her blood. It couldn't be something that Hugh had to do very often but he made it look easy, from putting in some local anaesthetic to find a vessel that was much deeper than a vein, inserting the cannula and then controlling the spurt of blood under pressure as he attached and taped down the Luer plug. He filled a tiny, two-ml syringe with the arterial blood.

'I'll page Janet or Tim to pop in and show you how to use the benchtop ABG analysis,' he told Lisa when he headed back to his other patient a few minutes later. 'We're also going to need a hand for a while. Might see what Peter's up to. I need to get Jim's blood pressure down so we'll have two patients that need close monitoring for some time.' He held her gaze. 'We could be in for a long night.'

'I wasn't planning on being anywhere else,' she responded.

Except that was only partly true. She might have been planning to be with Hugh tonight but it hadn't occurred to her that they might not be able to leave the medical centre and spend any time alone together. Not that it mattered. Except that that was only partly true also. There was no question that their patients had complete priority while they were on duty, but they only had a very limited number of nights left that they could find that kind of private time so losing one of them was actually quite a big deal. It felt as if there was a giant clock nearby that might be invisible but Lisa could hear the loudness of its ticking slowly increasing.

She was the kind of person you would want right by your side in any crisis but Hugh had already known that, hadn't he? It was one of those trustworthy things about Lisa Phillips. Like the way she had devoted herself to caring for her sister. And the way she not only always gave a hundred and ten percent in everything she did but she did it with intelligence and good-humoured grace even when she had to be rather tired by now.

Hugh was feeling a little weary himself. They'd put in quite a few miles of uphill walking today and work had been full on ever since the start of the evening surgery. They'd been kept very busy, despite calling in the extra team members, until the surgery hours were over. Now he and Lisa were alone in the medical centre and ship's hospital. Janet had gone to bed and Peter and Tim were going to be on call for anything else that happened on board overnight.

Jim's blood pressure had responded well to the intravenous medications and had dropped slowly enough not to cause any complications. Hugh wanted to keep him under observation till morning but he didn't need to be wakened for another check for an hour so he was sleeping peacefully. His wife had gone back to their cabin.

Michelle's condition had, thankfully,

started to improve once the extra medications had taken effect. Hugh wasn't going to let her go in a hurry either. He was going to keep a very careful eye on her blood oxygen levels, which meant another arterial sample needed to be taken soon and they would continue to give her both oxygen and nebuliser therapy every few hours.

The roll of the ship was more obvious now as the night wore on. It didn't bother Hugh at all—he rather liked a bit of rough water, in fact, and he had been pleased to see that it didn't seem to be affecting Lisa either. He was concerned about what her level of fatigue must be like by now, though, so he went to the tiny kitchen in the medical centre on the other side of the reception area and put the electric jug on to boil water so he could make Lisa a mug of coffee.

He left the door behind him ajar because this room was not much bigger than a cupboard and, as he gathered the mugs and spoons he needed, he could hear that someone had come into the reception area. He turned his head so that he could see through the crack of the door, hoping that it wasn't a new patient arriving. It wasn't. Lisa had obviously come out of the treatment room so as not to disturb Michelle by taking a phone call.

'I can't talk long,' she was saying. 'I'm monitoring a patient. What on earth are you doing up at this time of night anyway?'

Hugh heard the soft ping of the jug announcing that the water had boiled. He should step out of the room, he thought, and let Lisa know he was nearby. But he hesitated, probably because it was a little disturbing how much he wanted to step closer to her, having heard that note of anxiety in her voice. The urge to protect this woman and to fix things that might be a problem for her was getting steadily more pronounced.

'I told you not to open that mail, Abby.'

There was a note of something like panic in Lisa's voice now, even though she had lowered it, and that need to try and make things better for her was so powerful it squeezed his chest tightly enough to be a physical pain.

'It's not a problem, okay?' Her voice was firm now after a short silence. 'I'm dealing with it. That's why this job was such a great idea.'

Hugh could feel a deep frown creasing his forehead. What wasn't a problem? And why would being on this cruise be a way of dealing with it? Was there something she'd needed to get away from for a while? Or some*one*?

'It's only money,' he heard her say then. 'I've got this—I've got a plan. Don't worry. Look, I'll be home in just a couple of days and I'll explain everything. Now, I've really got to go. Talk soon, yeah?'

Lisa had her back to the kitchen door and she walked back to the treatment room as soon as she'd ended the call so she had no idea that Hugh had been eavesdropping.

He couldn't tell her, of course. Which meant he couldn't ask her what kind of problem she had or what the solution she was planning was all about. If it was money she needed, he had more than enough. He could help…

Or maybe not. Maybe he shouldn't try to find out what was going on and risk getting sucked into an even deeper involvement in Lisa's life.

It had been the mention of money that was changing things. Setting off warning bells that he couldn't ignore, despite the fact that they were taking him straight back to a place he had no desire to be. Back to those dismal days right before the wedding that had never happened. Back to the time when he'd lost both his fiancée and his best friend in one fell swoop.

Back to the worst moment of all. When Catherine had turned away from him to walk out of his life for ever with the words that were going to haunt him for ever.

'I never really loved *you*, Hugh. I just loved your money.'

CHAPTER EIGHT

THE STORM BUILT through the night.

By the time daylight broke, the huge ship was riding some dramatic swells that only seemed to get bigger as the day wore on. The Lido deck was closed and the view from the windows was of a such a dark grey sea it was almost black, so the contrast of the white foam of countless breaking waves was even more breathtaking. The feeling of your stomach dropping when a swell had been crested was alarming and the crunch of the change at the bottom before another climb was also breathtaking. Wind howled through windows that weren't closed tightly enough and people were tilted sideways as they negotiated corridors around the ship.

It was like riding a roller-coaster in very slow motion and Lisa had never wanted to ride any kind of roller-coaster. Or do any thrill seeking, for that matter. Hugh, on the other hand, was actually enjoying this.

The medical centre was busier than Lisa had ever seen and, despite having only managing to catch a few hours of interrupted sleep after caring for their inpatients overnight, she and Hugh were there along with Peter, Janet and Tim, dealing with not only the normal kind of workload but minor injuries that were arriving at an increasing rate due mainly to falls caused by the ship's rolling. They were also handing out huge quantities of anti-motion-sickness medications, trying to reassure overly anxious passengers, and they still had their inpatients.

Michelle seemed to be well over her frightening asthma attack but, for everybody's peace of mind, they were going to keep monitoring her for a few more hours. Jim's blood pressure was down to an acceptable level and he could be discharged as soon as a crew member was available to make sure he got back to his cabin safely.

On top of what was keeping the medical

centre so busy, they were also fielding calls to various parts of the ship. Tim had just rushed off to a cabin where it sounded like an elderly person had fallen and hit their head to cause a frightening amount of bleeding when another call came in.

'It's in the gym,' Hugh announced. 'Another fall but they're having trouble breathing so I might need a hand.'

Lisa came out from behind the desk instantly. She was on Hugh's watch so it was obvious that she was the one to accompany Hugh.

But he wasn't even looking in her direction. 'Janet?'

Janet put her hands up in front of her. 'Not unless I have to. I'm okay here but if I go forward and that high I'll get sick.' She was the one to turn to Lisa. 'You're not prone to motion sickness, are you?'

'Haven't noticed anything yet.' Lisa tried to smile but there *was* a knot in her stomach that could turn into nausea down the track. Anxiety about the storm had just been augmented by anxiety about why Hugh had chosen Janet to go with him rather than her.

'Be a good test for you, then.' Hugh still wasn't looking at Lisa as he picked up another one of their first response packs. 'The gym's right at the bow. And we need to cross the Lido deck if we want to get there fast. Here, put this on.' He handed Lisa a bright yellow sou'wester. 'Even if it's not raining, there's enough spray to get you soaked almost instantly.'

They needed to get there fast if someone was having difficulty breathing and that meant running up the stairs to avoid both waiting for an elevator and the risk of getting caught if there was a power outage.

There were people pressed against windows as they reached the interior part of the Lido deck and the collective cries of mixed awe, alarm and excitement only added to Lisa's anxiety.

'You ready?' Hugh had his shoulder against the door that led to the deck. 'Brace yourself.'

They only had about twenty metres to go

to get to the outside entrance of the gym on the other side of one of the swimming pools. Lisa was unprepared for the blast of wind as she went outside, however, and could feel herself losing her footing. She could get blown overboard, she thought. Or into a swimming pool that currently looked like something out of one of those horrific videos she'd seen where the grand piano was flying across a room. The water in the pool was tipping towards one end and then sloshing back to form a small tsunami that spilled out and washed across the deck with enough force to send deck chairs sliding into a heap against the railing.

For one terrible moment Lisa thought she might be going to drown and all she could think of was that she wouldn't be there for Abby when she was needed in the future. It had been bad enough not to have been there for her sister the other day when the upsetting incident with the patient had happened but at least she'd been able to talk to her and it had been enough. Not being there in any form would be even more of a failure than having been responsible for Abby's injuries in the first place.

How could she have been so irresponsible to have put herself in danger like this?

Except, in that same terrible moment, Hugh reached out and caught Lisa's arm. He was leaning into the wind and she could feel how stable his body was. He'd done this before. He was, in fact—judging by the grin on his face and the sparkle in his eyes—loving every moment of it.

Nothing could have demonstrated more clearly that they were—as Hugh had commented on during that, oh, so romantic dinner when they'd decided they could be friends—total opposites when it came to their approach to life.

But... Lisa was clinging to Hugh until they reached the doors that led to the relative safety of the gym. Opposites attracted, didn't they? Sometimes they could even make a long-term relationship work. If both sides wanted it to work, that was.

It was feeling more and more like Hugh was losing interest, however. Something was very different today but it wasn't until they were halfway through assessing the crew member in the gym who'd lost his balance and gone rolling across the floor to land against the metal handles of a piece of equipment that Lisa realised what it was.

The feeling of connection had vanished. As suddenly as a switch being flicked off.

Ever since their first night together, they'd been playing that game when they were working together. Frequent eye contact that was held just short of being a beat too long. Accentuating the kind of situations that meant they came into physical contact with each other, like their hands brushing when Lisa helped to shift the crew member's shirt to expose the painful area of his chest.

The tingle had gone. That awareness. Something was broken and Lisa didn't know what it was but it scared her. Okay, she'd known that her time with Hugh was coming to an end and it would be difficult but she'd thought they would make the most of it for as long as possible and then part as close friends. That they could stay in touch and might even see each other again one day. But maybe that was breaking some unspoken rule. That what happened on board ship simply ceased to exist when the cruise was over, and perhaps Hugh was thinking it was a good idea to wind things down as preparation so he wouldn't have to deal with tears or something when they said goodbye.

Or maybe what was really scaring her was being out in the open sea in weather like this. She could understand now why Janet had wanted to stay in the centre of the ship. Right up at the bow like this made the falling into the trough of a swell even more stomach-dropping and she could see the impressive wall of spray that came up to flood a lower deck when they hit the bottom of the dip between waves.

'Try and take a deep breath for me,' Hugh told their patient as he gently palpated an area where bruising was already becoming evident.

'Can't.' The young man's voice was strained. 'Hurts... *Ow...*'

'Sorry, mate. I think you might have

cracked a rib or two. Let me listen to your chest and then we'll give you something for the pain and get you down to the clinic so we can so some X-rays.' He unhooked the stethoscope from around his neck. 'You didn't hit your head as well, did you?' He looked up at another member of the gym staff. 'Was he knocked out?'

The other personal trainer shook his head. 'He just went flying, along with a bunch of gear. We've closed the gym now, which is a shame, because we're going to be stuck at sea for an extra day. Have you heard that Sardinia's been cancelled? We're heading straight back to Malaga.'

What a way to end a cruise.

You had to feel sorry for the passengers but, for Hugh, it was a blessing. He loved being flat out like this, facing a challenge that threatened to tip them past the point of being able to cope. He loved the thrill of riding waves like this but, best of all, it was the perfect excuse to totally ignore the mixed messages in his head concerning Lisa.

He was being given the chance to step right back and see what was going on from a perspective that wasn't getting sabotaged by spending personal time with her. Just being alone with Lisa was enough to make him want to trust her. Enough to make it preferable to block his ears to any alarm bells ringing. It was a bonus that fate was going to ensure they didn't get a chance to make love again because that would be even harder to resist and might make him want really stupid things, like being able to wake up with her in his bed for the rest of his life.

How could you feel so strongly about someone you'd only met a couple of weeks ago? He didn't really know Lisa at all, did he? Not that it probably made much difference in the long run. He'd known Catherine for two years, for heaven's sake.

As another bonus, there were the other medical staff around. It was Tim who helped Hugh glue the scalp wound that he'd found on the patient who'd been bleeding in her cabin. Peter took the X-rays that confirmed the broken ribs that the personal trainer had suffered but had also been reassuring that there was no underlying injury like a punctured lung.

He also X-rayed a Colles' wrist fracture that came in a little later and Lisa was tasked with helping splint the arm with a plaster slab underneath which kept her well out of Hugh's way for some time.

He hadn't missed the occasional puzzled glance that came his way from her from time to time but it was as though he wasn't actually in control of the growing distance between them. It was simply happening and he wasn't exactly enjoying the process himself.

He was missing Lisa already.

The medical staff took turns to have meal breaks by themselves or had food delivered by room service to ensure that they were caring for their inpatients, that someone was available at all times to see people that turned up at the clinic and that they had enough staff to respond to calls from other parts of the ship as well.

That would need to continue overnight, although the forecast was that the weather would have settled by the time they were due to dock in Malaga tomorrow morning. Even if that was the case, however, everybody was going to be exhausted by the time they reached their final port but at least Hugh and the rest of the team would have a couple of days off before a new cruise began—a three-week one next time—and Lisa would be heading home and would no doubt have plenty of time to rest before going back to her real job.

And her real life that didn't include him. Maybe it couldn't include any permanent relationship given that her sister was her first priority. Ironically, that was one of the things he loved about Lisa. The thing that made him feel like she was completely trustworthy and that was what was doing his head in enough to make it impossible to sleep when he was given a break in the early hours of the morning.

Instead, he went walking around the ship because, finally, the seas around them were subsiding. He might as well get a coffee, Hugh decided, because there was little point in trying to sleep for what was left of the night. They would be busy as soon as they docked as well, making arrangements for transport for the people who needed hospital care, like the woman who'd broken her wrist.

There were staff in the bar on the Lido deck that was now open again and it seemed like something was drawing Hugh into it.

'Just a coffee, thanks, mate.'

'Bet you've been busy, Doc. It's been kind of a wild ride, hasn't it?'

'You're not wrong there. Just as well you were closed for the day, I think. You've had enough drama in this bar for one cruise.'

Hugh took the coffee but decided not to stay on the bar stool to drink it. The reminder of the drama in this bar early on in this cruise was a reminder of something else and he was too weary to cope with any addition to the confusion he had going on in his head. It had been right here when he'd first properly worked with Lisa Phillips as they'd responded to the crisis of Alex's anaphylactic reaction. He'd never be able to come into this bar again without thinking of her, would he?

He walked to the edge of the deck instead and stood by the rail. He could see down onto a lower deck from here and there were obviously plenty of crew working overtime tonight to start the clean-up process that was part of the aftermath of bad weather. The kitchens and dining rooms would be even worse than the decks. Hugh had already treated a few lacerations from people dealing with bucketloads of broken glass. The deck chairs were one of the main issues outside. They got blown around or washed into corners to end up in a tangled heap. Someone was walking around one of those piles right now. A small figure in a bright yellow sou'wester.

Lisa…

Was she on the way to a call or just getting some fresh air? Hugh leaned over the rail, tempted to call out. Tempted to invite her to come and have a coffee with him just because he wanted to be closer to her. As he opened his mouth, however, he saw Lisa turn suddenly and then stoop to pick something up from amongst the jumble of deck-chair legs.

It was a wallet. He might be well above Lisa and it was the middle of the night but she was standing directly beneath a light so it was easy to see just how full of notes that wallet was when she opened it to have a look, and then touched the wad of notes as if trying to estimate its value. Hugh could also see the astonishment on Lisa's face and the way she instantly looked around, as if she expected the owner of the wallet to be nearby. Or was she wondering if anyone had seen her? The only person on that section of the deck was a crew member who had his arms full of folded deck chairs and he was walking away from Lisa to join his colleagues so he hadn't seen her. She looked over her shoulder again and then, with what almost looked like a shrug of her shoulders, Lisa folded the wallet and slipped it into the pocket of her coat.

He knew perfectly well that Lisa wasn't stealing that wallet. That she would be taking it to someone who would know what to do about finding its owner. He knew that with the same conviction that he knew how much she loved her sister. What that little scenario did do, however, was give Hugh a glimpse of an escape route back to a safe place. Because he had buttons that could be pushed quite easily when it came to women who cared too much about money—buttons that had clearly already been primed by overhearing that conversation Lisa had had with her sister. And because that button being pushed automatically pushed another one, that made him also easily remember the pain of making oneself vulnerable by loving someone so much that they had the power to break your heart.

That kind of pain was what was very likely to happen if he allowed this fling with Lisa to get any bigger than it already was. He could get hurt again. And, if that wasn't enough to convince him to pull the plug on what was happening between them, there was something else that was even less acceptable. Lisa was going to get hurt. And,

okay, she might be going to get hurt anyway but this was about damage limitation
now, wasn't it? For her sake even more than
his own. Because that's what you did when
you cared enough about someone else. They
would both get over this. It had just been a
shipboard fling, after all.

It wasn't exactly the end to this cruise that
Lisa had imagined or that she would have
wished for.

She was on deck as dawn was breaking
and this massive ship was edging into port
at Malaga. In a matter of only a few hours,
she would be walking down the gangway
and away from the most extraordinary job
she'd ever had.

Away from the most extraordinary man
she'd ever met.

She'd hardly seen him since that storm had
peaked and they'd gone to that call in the
gym together. She'd known that something
had changed but she couldn't understand
why. Unless she'd been completely wrong
in the kind of man she believed Hugh Pat-

terson to be? Maybe that very first impression of him had been the correct one. That he was one of those shallow, wealthy, pleasure-seeking people who were up for unlimited sexual adventures with no intention of getting involved or thought of hurting others along the way.

No…that wasn't going to work. She knew perfectly well that Hugh was one of the most genuine and caring people she'd ever met.

In fact…that was Hugh walking towards her right now and the expression on his face was exactly that. Genuine. Caring. She knew that her own face must be showing a lot of what was happening inside her. Joy in seeing him but puzzlement about why he'd apparently been avoiding her. A need to snatch any last moments they could enjoy together but sadness in knowing that they *would* be the last.

Maybe Hugh could see all that and maybe that was why there was no need to say anything. Why he took her into his arms as she turned away from the rail towards him. Why he kissed her with such…thoroughness…

But it felt different. So heartbreakingly tender it could have been a final farewell.

Somebody walked past, which was enough to make them break the kiss, but Lisa couldn't bear to move out of the circle of his arms yet so she put her head into the hollow of his shoulder, where she could hear the beat of his heart. The way she had done many times now, when they were in bed together and desire had been sated, at least temporarily.

'I feel like I haven't seen you for so long already,' she murmured. 'I was missing you, Hugh.'

'I was up here a few hours ago.' Hugh's voice was a rumble beneath her ear. He sounded incredibly weary. Almost sad, in fact. 'I saw you on the lower deck. It looked like you'd dropped something?'

'Not me.' Lisa closed her eyes so she could soak in how it felt to have Hugh's arms around her like this. 'Somebody must have lost their wallet in the storm. It's crazy how much money some people carry around with them.' Not that Lisa wanted to talk about this. There were far more important things she wanted to talk about. Like whether or not she might ever see Hugh again. 'I… um…handed it in.'

'Oh…' It seemed like Hugh's grip tightened around her for a moment but then he let her go. 'Of course you did.'

There was something odd in his tone. Something that made Lisa look up to catch his gaze, and she couldn't interpret what she could see in his eyes but it looked as if it was mostly something sad. Disappointed even?

Perhaps he was feeling the same way she was. That she was about to lose something very precious. Lisa took a deep breath and summoned every bit of courage she had.

'I'm going to miss you, Hugh,' she whispered. 'I… I love you…'

He held her gaze. She could see the way his face softened as he smiled. 'I'm going to miss you, too, Lisa. It's been fun, hasn't it?'

Lisa swallowed hard. *Fun*?

He wasn't going to say it back, was he?

Because he didn't feel the same way. He'd just been having *fun*… Already she could feel the rush of blood to her cheeks. The heat of mortification…

Hugh broke their gaze to look over the railings of the deck. 'We'll be finished docking soon,' he said quietly. 'Our cruise will be officially over.'

And the cruise wasn't the only thing that would be officially over, obviously. Lisa was cringing inside now and she knew she must be the colour of a beetroot by now. She'd just told this man she loved him and he was about to tell her that he never wanted to see her again?

'I know,' she said quickly. 'And it'll be time to say goodbye. These cruise things… well, they're like holiday flings, I guess. Better to leave them as a good memory than turn them into dust by trying to make them into something they're not, yes?'

Why on earth was she trying to make this so easy for him? Or was it that she was just trying to make it less painful for herself? To give herself a chance to get away before he could see just how devastating this was for her?

'Especially for people like us.' Hugh's tone seemed to hold a sigh of relief. 'You're a family person through and through. It's been hard for you to be away from your sister, hasn't it? Me—I could never stay in one place for long.'

Or with one person. Lisa could easily add those unspoken words. She'd known that right from the start. Had she really thought that maybe she would be the one to change his mind?

She really did have to escape.

'I'd better go and start packing.' She actually managed to sound cheerful. Excited about the prospect of going home, even? 'I'll come down to the clinic to say goodbye properly before I go onshore.'

Hugh wasn't in the clinic when Lisa went in to make her farewells. He had intended to be there, of course—it was the polite thing to do—but he'd left it too late because he'd gone back to that bar on the Lido deck now that he was off duty, to do something he would never normally do at this time of day.

'Another coffee, Doc?'

'No. I've been up for so long it doesn't feel like morning any more. I'll have a glass of champagne, thanks.'

Because, in defeat, you needed it?

So here he was, watching the swarm of people leaving the ship far below him, with his glass almost empty, and that was when he realised he'd left it too late to say goodbye properly to Lisa Phillips, because he could see her on the pier, dragging her bright red suitcase behind her as she headed for the taxi rank.

She'd told him she loved him.

And he'd had to exert every ounce of his strength not to say it back. If he had, they would have stayed there in each other's arms, making plans for a future together that could never have worked. This was the life he loved and he was nowhere near ready to give it up. Lisa would never want to work on a cruise ship on a more permanent basis because that would take her away from her beloved sister. A sister who needed her to be close because she was disabled. He couldn't compete with that although Lisa might have agreed to work at sea with him if he'd asked. Because she loved him and he could feel the truth of that in a way he never had with the woman he'd almost married.

And he loved her which was why he'd pushed her away. Because if you felt like that about someone, you did what was best for them, not for yourself. He could never ask Lisa to give up caring for her sister to be with him. No matter how much she loved him, a part of her would be miserable and that would undermine everything. He would hate himself for making her miserable and maybe she would even hate him in the end. And, if he'd given up the life he loved in order to be with her, he would have been miserable and the end result would have been the same. It could never have worked so it was better this way. It just didn't feel like it yet.

It was easy to recognise Lisa down there on the pier but Hugh knew she wouldn't be able to spot him. It felt like she could, though, when he saw the way she stopped and turned to stare up at the ship for the longest moment.

It felt like a piece of his heart was tearing off.

CHAPTER NINE

ABIGAIL PHILLIPS WAS increasingly worried about her older sister.

She could understand that there would be a period of readjustment from the excitement of that amazing couple of weeks she'd had working on a cruise ship and then having to settle into a new job as a junior care home manager but it had been another couple of weeks now and, as far as Abby could tell, this new job was a complete disaster.

She'd never seen Lisa looking so miserable.

In an effort to cheer her up, Abby had not only picked up their takeaway dinner, in what they'd agreed would be a weekly tradition now that they weren't living together, she had a special gift for Lisa.

'Put the food in the kitchen and we'll heat

it up soon. Come and sit in the lounge with me. I've got something for you.'

An advantage to being in a wheelchair was that you could tuck things in beside you and keep them hidden. It was a little harder with the bottle-shaped something that Abby had on her left side but she'd hidden that with her big, soft shoulder bag. The small, flat package on her right side had been easier to conceal.

Lisa opened the wrapping and then froze as she stared at what was inside the package. Abby's heart sank like a stone.

'It's that French café,' she said. 'The one you sent me the picture of. I thought you'd like a memory of being in the most romantic place on earth.' And that was why she'd chosen a silver frame with heart-shaped corners for the print of Lisa, sitting beneath grapevines, with the most beautiful view in the background, holding up a glass of champagne in a toast, she'd later labelled *Here's to living the dream!* when she'd sent it to Abby. Seeing even an echo of that kind of joyous smile on her face was what Abby had been aiming for this evening. What actually happened was that Lisa burst into tears.

'Oh, heck...' Abby manoeuvred her chair and put the brakes on so that she could transfer herself to the couch and put her arms around her sister. 'I'm sorry... I've done the wrong thing, haven't I?'

'It's not you.' Lisa was making a valiant effort to stifle her sobs. She scrubbed at her eyes and sniffed. 'I...love the photo...'

'It's that new job of yours, isn't it? I know you hate it.'

'It's not that bad.'

'But you hate it, don't you?'

'I just need to get used to it. Being in an office that doesn't even have a window instead of working with any patients myself, you know? The closest I get is helping the family fill in their pre-admission forms or organising medical appointments for the residents that can't be managed in our treatment rooms.'

'You'd rather be back on that ship? Dealing with exciting things like that guy who stopped breathing? Going to romantic places like this café?'

But Lisa was shaking her head with such emphasis that it was almost despair and Abby finally twigged.

'Oh…my God,' she breathed. 'You *did* have a fling with that cute doctor, didn't you? That was why you started looking like a kid on Christmas morning.'

Lisa caught a slow tear that was trickling down the side of her nose. 'It was a really bad idea. I knew what he was like. The first time I ever saw him he was kissing another woman, for heaven's sake.'

'He *cheated* on you?' Abby could feel a knot of anger forming in her gut. Whatever the guy had done, he'd hurt Lisa and that was unforgivable.

'You can't cheat on someone if you're not in a relationship,' Lisa said. 'And we weren't. We both knew it was only going to last as long as the cruise and, no, I know that he wasn't interested in anyone else while he was with me. He just…switched off being interested in me at the end. Like it hadn't been anything important...or even special...'

Abby watched as Lisa screwed her eyes tightly shut to try and ward off any more tears. 'You fell in love with him, didn't you?' Her own heart was breaking for Lisa. 'You went for the first non-boring guy ever and you fell for him.'

Lisa nodded miserably. 'It was entirely my fault. I knew it wasn't safe. I knew I was playing with fire and there was a good chance I'd get burnt. And that's exactly what happened.'

'Takes two to tango,' Abby muttered.

'It wasn't as if it was anything that could have become something more and we both knew that. That day, in that café in the picture, we'd agreed we could be friends even if we were total opposites and then...and then he made me laugh when I was feeling really crap.'

Abby shook her head. 'Yeah, that'll do it. What is it that's so powerful about someone making you laugh?'

'Maybe it's because it's something that

shows you want someone to feel better. And that there has to be a connection, whether you've known it was there or not, to make it work.'

'Hmm...you could be right.' But Abby frowned. 'Why were you feeling so crap?'

'We'd lost a patient. A cardiac arrest in a guy who was on his honeymoon. We tried to resuscitate him for nearly an hour but we were never going to win.'

Abby's eyes widened. 'You never told me about that.'

'Well, you were having a hard time yourself. It was the same day that you'd had that patient assume *you* were a patient as well, not his therapist.'

'Oh...so you were already feeling bad and then I heaped all my crap on you and you spent your time trying to make me feel better but didn't even let me know how you were feeling so I couldn't try to make *you* feel better.' Abby really was angry now. 'How do you think that makes *me* feel?' She reached to pull her chair closer, intending to get off the couch and away from Lisa before they revisited an argument that would ruin the evening—the one about how Lisa had always done too much for Abby, who was never allowed to reciprocate in any meaningful way. 'And, as for that guy, what was his name?'

'Hugh…' Lisa's voice was a whisper.

'Yeah… *Hugh…* Well, he's just a bastard and you're better off a million miles away from him. Man, I wish I could tell him exactly what I think of him.'

It wasn't possible to shift herself onto the cushion of her chair until she'd pulled her shoulder bag off the cushion. Oh…and that bottle of champagne. She would have hidden it from Lisa but it was too late. She'd seen it and she was crying again. But she was laughing through her tears and suddenly that made the prospect of a big fight evaporate instantly. It was Lisa who put her arms around Abby this time, to give her a fierce hug. They'd been through far worse times than this and survived. They would always survive because they had each other as support, even if the giving had always been too heavily weighted on Lisa's side.

'How did you know?' Lisa asked when she finally pulled herself free of the hug and wiped her eyes.

'Know what?'

'That, in defeat, you need champagne.'

'What on earth are you talking about, Lise?'

Lisa got to feet. 'I'll find some glasses,' she said. 'And then give you a wee history lesson about Napoleon Bonaparte.'

'It's lovely to see you, Hugh. Or it would be, if you weren't looking so...wrecked.'

'You mean I look older?' Hugh shrugged. 'It's the end of a three-weeker and we had some challenging passengers on board. Hypochondriacs, mostly. Very demanding ones.'

He hadn't enjoyed the last three weeks nearly as much as he usually enjoyed his job but maybe that was due to the fact that he'd enjoyed the previous cruise so much more than normal—up until the end of it, anyway.

Because he had been sharing it with Lisa and that had made everything seem new and far more meaningful. He'd taken her to some of his favourite places. Worse, he'd taken her to his bed and the effect of sharing that with Lisa had been the same. New. Far more meaningful.

But he'd been right to let her walk back to her own life without the complications that would have come if they'd tried to keep their connection. Lisa wasn't the kind of woman who'd be happy to see him for an afternoon here or there when he happened to be in London. She deserved someone who could offer her the same kind of loyalty and commitment that she would give to someone she loved. The kind she was already committed to giving to Abby who—as she'd said herself—was the most important person in her life.

It should have been a lot easier than this to have turned back to embrace the lifestyle that had been so perfect for the last couple of years. Not much more than a month ago he'd been looking forward to spending an afternoon with Carlotta in Barcelona. He could remember how much he had enjoyed kissing her and maybe that's what he really needed to distract him. Hugh raised his hand to signal the waiter that he was ready to pay the bill for their lunch. Now they could go somewhere more appropriate for some more intimate time together.

He found what he hoped was a seductive smile, although it felt rather more that he was leering at his companion.

'You, on the other hand, look as gorgeous as ever, Carlotta. Shall we go somewhere more comfortable?'

'Of course…' But Carlotta was looking at his full glass. 'You don't want to finish your wine first?'

'I think I might have gone off champagne.' There were too many memories associated with it now, that was the problem, and every one of them included Lisa Phillips.

So many wonderful memories, like the way she would glow with the pleasure and wonder of a new experience, like tasting champagne for the first time or soaking in a fabulous view or enjoying a delicious meal or...or...dear Lord...the way she used to look when she was coming apart in his arms...

Man, it was hot here today. Hugh was wearing an open-necked shirt and yet he had an urge to loosen his tie or go in search of a sea breeze. Was his face as red as it felt? Surely he wasn't blushing, the way Lisa had been unable to prevent herself doing so furiously when she was uncomfortable or embarrassed. Like the way her cheeks had gone such a bright colour after she'd told him she loved him and he hadn't said it back...

Okay...knowing that he'd hurt Lisa wasn't such a good memory. But neither was the one that sprang to mind when Hugh opened his wallet to extract a note or two to leave a tip for their waiter. It was sad, he decided as he put his hand on Carlotta's lower back to guide her between tables, that it only took one less than happy memory to take the shine off so many of the better ones.

Carlotta slipped her arm around his waist as they left the restaurant and it was enough for him to stop and turn towards her. She put a hand on his cheek then and raised her face to kiss him. But Hugh found himself breaking the contact of their lips almost instantly. Lifting his head with a jerk.

'I'm sorry,' he said. 'But I can't… I don't know what's wrong with me today.'

'I think I do.' Carlotta's smile was knowing. 'I don't know who she is, but I think it's finally happened. You've fallen in love.'

Hugh shook his head. 'Nope. I did that once and it was the biggest mistake I ever made. I wouldn't be stupid enough to do it again.'

Carlotta's gaze was full of sympathy now. 'Oh, Hugh…it's not something you can stop happening. You can fight it, of course. Walk away from it even. But you never know… walking away from it this time might be an even bigger mistake than choosing the wrong person the first time.' She touched his cheek again before walking away with a wave. 'Thanks for lunch, Hugh. And best of luck…'

It wasn't far back to the ship and Hugh

walked briskly despite the heat of the Spanish afternoon. Simon was at his usual place at the bottom of the gangway, although it was only staff he was welcoming back on board today. The passengers from this cruise had all disembarked this morning.

'Hey, Hugh...how's it going? Happy to have a day off?'

'I've got a few days off this time. I'm thinking of grabbing a flight to London and visiting my folks.'

By the time he reached the marble-floored atrium, where Harry's piano was deserted and silent, the idea of escaping the ship for a few days had become so appealing that Hugh went towards one of the desks where he knew someone could help him make his travel arrangements. Everyone on board relied on Sally to answer any questions because she'd been in the business for so long she seemed to know everything. If she couldn't give you the answer herself, she always knew where to find it.

Hugh wasn't the only one with a query this afternoon. The ship's captain was ahead of him and as Hugh got closer he was startled to hear what the captain was saying.

'I'm sure her name was Lisa. She was wearing scrubs under her sou'wester, so I assume she was working in the medical centre. It was the night of that storm.'

'Oh, I remember.' Sally nodded. 'That was some storm. Now…let me look and see if I can find who she was.'

'Lisa Phillips,' Hugh told them. 'She was just a locum nurse—only with us for the one cruise.'

Just…? Lisa could never be "just" anything. She was an extraordinary human being, that's what she was…and Carlotta was right. He *was* in love with her. She had been in love with him and had been brave enough to tell him. And he had thrown that back in her face. Even if he'd had good reason, which he'd believed he did, it was a horrible thing to have done. He hadn't even said goodbye to her, had he?

'Well, I need her address,' the captain said. 'I've got a rather large cheque to forward.'

Hugh blinked. Sally looked curious as well. 'Whatever for?' she asked.

'Someone lost their wallet during that storm. This Lisa found it and handed it in. Well, she bumped into me and asked me where she could find someone from Security and I said I'd look after it for her. We tracked down the owner once things had settled down and, after he got home, he was so impressed that the wallet had still had a rather ill-advised amount of cash in it that he thought the person who'd found it deserved a reward.'

Hugh's breath caught in his throat. Lisa not only deserved an apology from him, she deserved the reward of that cheque. And… it gave him a perfect excuse to see her again.

He cleared his throat. 'I'm about to head to London for a day or two,' he said. 'I could deliver it personally, perhaps, if she's not too far away?'

'Marvellous idea.' The captain handed him the envelope. 'Get some flowers to go with it, lad, and tell her that we all appreciate her honesty. She's done our reputation a power of good.'

Sally was beaming. 'Let me find her address in the system for you. Ooh, I'd love to be a fly on the wall when you turn up on her doorstep. Won't she be thrilled?'

Abby glared at the man on the doorstep.

She hadn't needed his introduction.

'I *know* who you are,' she said. 'Lisa's working late but even if she was home I'm pretty damn sure she wouldn't want to see you.'

Mind you, this ship's doctor was a lot cuter in real life than in that photo on the website. He also had a massive bunch of flowers in his arms and an expression in those rather gorgeous brown eyes that looked...nervous?

The flowers—and the man—were getting rapidly wetter as they stood there in the pouring rain but Abby suddenly had misgivings about whether sending this unexpected visitor instantly on his way was the right thing to do. Hadn't she wanted the opportunity to give him a piece of her mind about how he had treated her sister?

'You'd better come in for a minute,' she said ungraciously. 'I don't want those flowers dripping all over my lap.' Abby swung her chair around and headed for the kitchen. 'Put them in the sink,' she ordered. 'I'll deal with them later.'

He did as he was told, which was gratifying. But then he gave her a grin that was cheeky enough to disarm her completely.

'And there I was thinking that Lisa was the bossy sister,' he said.

Abby couldn't help a huff of laughter escaping. 'She is. It's actually very out of character for me to be rude but...'

'But...?'

'I don't like you,' Abby told him bluntly. 'You've made my sister miserable.'

'I'm really sorry about that. Maybe this will cheer her up.'

Hugh took an envelope out of his pocket and handed it to Abby, who opened it. Her jaw dropped when she saw the amount the cheque was written out for. By the time

Hugh had explained what it was for, she had a lump in her throat that made it difficult to swallow.

'She only took that job on the ship because she was desperate for a bit of extra money,' she told Hugh. 'Because of *me*... She got a loan to get a specially modified car for me but it was a real struggle for her to meet the payments, especially when she had to find a new job after being made redundant. She even missed a mortgage payment on the house—I opened a threatening letter from the bank when she was away, which was really scary. Anyway...' She put the cheque back into its envelope, so that Lisa could get the same surprise that she'd had. 'I shouldn't be telling you any of this but I guess it's just as much my fault as yours that she's miserable now.'

He didn't say anything but when Abby looked up, she could see how carefully he was listening. How important this was to him. He also looked as though he was concerned for Abby. Perhaps he could sense how close she was to crying?

'You'd better sit down,' she said. 'Would you like a cup of tea?'

'You knew about me, didn't you?' she asked a short time later as she put a mug of tea on the kitchen table in front of Hugh.

'I knew you'd had an accident when you were very young that left you in a wheelchair. That your sister is about six years older than you and is completely devoted to you and that she was worried about not living with you any more.'

'Did you know that she's my half-sister?'

Hugh nodded. 'She did tell me that. In almost the same breath that she told me how much she loves you.'

'So she didn't tell you that we had different fathers because my mother had drug and alcohol problems that meant her relationships never lasted? That Lisa was more of a mother to me than our mother ever was, even though she was only a kid herself? That she's always blamed herself for my accident because she wasn't holding my hand tightly enough and I escaped and ran out in front of a car?'

Again, Hugh said nothing. He looked as though he had no idea where to find the words he might need but Abby wasn't going to help him. He needed to know more.

'For her entire life she's put me first,' Abby said quietly. 'She's done it out of love but she's also done it out of guilt and that's something that's really hard for me to live with. She was only a kid herself, for God's sake. She's got nothing to feel guilty about but she chose her career so that she could stay close to home. She wanted to be a doctor but that would have meant going to a medical school away from home so she did nursing training instead.'

'I kind of guessed that.' Hugh nodded.

'She never went to parties when she was a teenager. Never spent money on herself or took a gap year to do any travelling. She took over the mortgage on this house when Gran died and said it was worth it because it would keep us safe. I reckon she chose her boring boyfriends because they were safe options that weren't going to interfere with her life. I don't believe she's ever been in love either. Until now. Which means this is her first broken heart and…and it might be *my* fault she met you in the first place but that…that's down to *you*…'

Again, Hugh nodded. 'It might not be my first broken heart,' he admitted. 'But it feels like it is. And I can't argue with you because it is down to me. I've wrecked the most amazing thing I've ever found and I have no idea what to do about it. I'm sure you're probably also right about Lisa not wanting to see me.'

'Are you saying what I think you're saying?' Abby waited for Hugh to meet her gaze so that she could gauge how genuine he might be. 'That you're in love with Lise? That you really *want* to be with her?'

'For the rest of my life,' Hugh said softly. 'I'm never going to meet anyone else like your sister. I don't think there *is* anyone else in the world that lights up when she's happy quite like Lisa does. I want to see her that happy for the rest of *her* life. I want to be the one who creates some of that happiness.'

'Oh, my God…' Abby could feel a tear

sneaking down her cheek. 'That's exactly what I want for her, too.'

'I'm not.' Hugh held up his hands in a gesture of surrender. 'And I realise now that being with Lisa is more important than a lifestyle that isn't exactly compatible with a long term future. I understand how important you are to her, too. I totally respect that. I love that she loves you that much.'

Abby swiped at the moisture on her cheeks. 'I'm perfectly capable of being independent, thank you. I've *told* her that. I've told her that if she wants to go and have an exciting job at sea instead of the one she hates so much here, then I might miss her but I'd be fine. I need to be independent.' Abby had found a shaky smile. 'You'd be doing me a favour if you persuaded her to go sailing off into the sunset with you for a good, long while. You can always settle down later, you know.'

'I don't think I'd be able to do that.' Hugh was shaking his head. 'She's a determined woman, your sister, and I've hurt her. It's going to take something pretty special to get her to even listen to me, isn't it?'

'Hmm…' Abby had no doubts at all about how genuine Hugh Patterson was. She could also see exactly why her sister had fallen in love with this man. But he was right. Lisa thought she had played with fire and been burnt. She wouldn't be keen to go anywhere near that heat again.

Her gaze drifted over to the flowers in the kitchen sink. And then it lifted to the window sill above them, which was where Lisa had put the small framed photo that Abby had given her last week. She turned slowly back to her guest. Biting her lip couldn't stop the smile that wanted to escape.

'I think I might have an idea,' she said.

CHAPTER TEN

'I CAN'T BELIEVE I let you talk me into this.'

'Shh… I'm busy.'

Lisa had to smile at the expression on Abby's face as her sister closed her eyes for a moment. It was sheer bliss, that's what it was.

'You don't look very busy.'

'I am. It's a big deal, you know—this living the dream stuff.'

'I know…' Her voice cracked with the emotion of it because this was exactly what she'd dreamed of for Abby, only a matter of a few weeks ago. For her to be here. In this exact spot. At this precise table, in fact, that had the best view from the terrace.

Not that she'd made it easy. Even after the astonishing good fortune of Abby winning those tickets for a weekend in the South of

France in some radio competition—on top of that amazing reward that had been delivered with some flowers on behalf of the ship's captain—Lisa had initially totally refused to give in to Abby's plea to experience the most romantic place on earth. She'd even taken that photograph off the kitchen windowsill and hidden it in a drawer so she didn't have to think about it every time she caught a glimpse of the image.

'It's the last place on earth I'd want to go,' she'd said. *'I can't believe you'd even ask.'*

'It's not as though you were there on a date,' Abby had pointed out. *'It was before you hooked up with Hugh, remember? You were there as friends and you look so happy in that photo. It might help.'*

'How?'

'Oh... I don't know. Like one of those reset things you can do on the computer. Where you can pick a time when you knew things were good and have all your settings revert to what they were then.' The look on Abby's face reminded Lisa of when she'd been a small child and had desperately wanted

something that she couldn't have or do because the wheelchair had made it too difficult. *'Please? For me?'*

So, of course, in the end she had agreed. When had she ever not agreed to something that Abby wanted so much?

She'd even let Abby choose her outfit. A floaty red dress sprinkled with tiny white flowers, white sandals and a little white flower on a hair clip. They might have very different shades of red hair themselves, with Lisa being a dark auburn and Abby much more of a strawberry blonde, but it had been a pact from when they were both children that they would wear red whenever they liked.

Abby's eyes opened again. 'Where's that champagne?' she asked.

'Relax. I'm sure it's on its way. We've got plenty of time. The car isn't coming back for us for hours. Have you decided what you want to eat yet?'

'I need some more time—it all looks so good. And I need to go to the loo before I think about it any more.'

'Oh...' Lisa's chair scraped on the stone of the floor. 'Of course...'

Abby's eyebrows shot up. '*You* need to go to the loo, too?'

'No... I thought...' Lisa sat down with a sigh. 'Sorry...'

'No problem.' Abby's smile was forgiving. 'And if I hadn't already checked out that they had a disabled toilet available I would probably be very grateful for your assistance. As it is, I can manage perfectly well on my own. So *you* relax. I'll be back soon.'

Watching her sister expertly manoeuvre between the tables, heading back to the reception area inside the café, Lisa managed to let go of the underlying anxiety that this might not have been a good idea. Abby had managed the travelling with ease and she was revelling in everything they had packed into this short getaway already. It had been such an amazing prize that had not only included a luxury hotel in Nice but a chauffeur-driven car for any sightseeing they had wanted to do.

Relaxing for a few minutes as she waited

for Abby to return wasn't difficult. It was even warmer than it had been the last time Lisa had been here so the soft breeze drifting over the canopy of the forest beneath the café was more than welcome. The shade from the grapevine running rampant over the pergola was just as welcome and the play of shadows from the sunlight finding gaps in the leaves was delightful. It would make it harder to see when Abby was coming back, although Lisa could see a waiter standing beside the bar, putting a bottle into an ice bucket. Their champagne? She hoped that Abby would return in time to see it being opened because that pop of the cork was all part of the magic, wasn't it?

Or it had been the last time.

The first time.

From the corner of her eye, Lisa could see the waiter approaching the table now. He had a white cloth over his arm, the bottle in the bucket in one hand and two fluted glasses in the other. It was impossible not to drift back in time. To remember what it was like when those thousands of tiny bubbles exploded in her mouth and then evaporated into delicious iciness. To remember opening her eyes to find Hugh staring at her with an intensity that had taken her breath away all over again.

The same way he'd looked at her when they had been making love…

She could even hear an echo of his voice—*'I knew you'd look like that'*—with that note of happiness because *she'd* been so happy.

Oh, help…

She wasn't going to cry, Lisa told herself firmly. She wasn't going to let anything spoil this for Abby. But where *was* Abby? She was taking such a long time—maybe she did need some help after all. Lisa had to peer past the waiter to try and see if Abby had appeared again yet.

'Don't worry, she's fine.'

Lisa's jaw dropped in total disbelief as she recognised the voice of the waiter and looked up.

Hugh's smile was reassuring but the cork shot from the bottle with a sound like gunfire that made Lisa jump. He caught the escaping foam in one of the glasses.

'It was all part of the plan.' Hugh's smile had disappeared as he slid into the seat on the other side of this small wrought-iron table.

'I've been a complete idiot,' he said quietly. 'Do you think you could ever forgive me?'

This was overwhelming. Lisa suspected she might look like a stone statue because that was how she was feeling. There were just too many feelings that were too powerful.

How much manipulation had gone on to entice her here for what had clearly been a set-up? For someone who'd kept such tight control of everything in her life, including herself—in order to keep Abby and herself safe—the idea that she had fallen for it was somehow shameful.

Knowing that her beloved sister had been in on it and had kept the secret so well was so surprising it was hurtful.

The fact that it was happening here, in what she herself had described as the most romantic place on earth, had the potential to take the magic away and make it simply a stage set and not real at all.

But running beneath that horrible mix of impressions that made her want to get to her feet and run was something else. A bright, shiny thread of what felt like hope. That something precious was about to be offered to her and all she had to do was to be brave enough to accept the gift.

Finally, she found her voice. 'Um…whose idea was this?'

'Abby's,' Hugh admitted. 'Although I have to say I thought it was brilliant and you know why?'

'Why?' There were plenty more questions to ask about how and why Abby had been colluding with Hugh but they could wait. There was something far more compelling about the expression in those brown eyes Lisa loved so much. Whatever he was about to say was so important he wasn't going to let her look away.

'Because this was where you had your first taste of champagne. Where I saw that joy of it in your face. And maybe I didn't realise it at the time—okay, I probably would have run a mile if I *had* realised it—but I think that was the moment I started to fall in love with you, Lisa.'

Oh, yes…that shiny thread of hope was glowing now. Shining so brightly that it was casting a shadow over everything else.

'I told Abby how much I was in love with you. That I want to see that kind of happiness in your face as often as possible for the rest of your life and that I want to be able to do whatever I can to create that happiness for you.' Hugh's voice cracked a little. 'And you know what she said?'

Lisa shook her head. She couldn't get any words past the lump in her throat.

'She said that she wants exactly the same thing. We're friends for life now, your sister and me.'

'Oh…' There was no stopping the tears that were determined to escape.

'She told me about what happened,' Hugh said gently. 'That you've always been so determined to look after her and keep her safe.

That you've held onto guilt for something that wasn't your fault.'

'But it was,' Lisa whispered. 'It was...' She swallowed hard. Maybe he didn't know the whole truth—the worst thing about her. 'There was a doll. In the toy shop window. A really beautiful doll with curly yellow hair and I was standing there, wishing with all my heart that I had hair like that and that I could take that doll home with me... That was when it happened. I let go of Abby's hand.'

'You didn't let go, sweetheart,' Hugh said softly. 'Abby pulled because she wanted to run. She took you by surprise. You were only a little girl yourself and you should never have been given that responsibility in the first place. You've always had too much responsibility and you've taken that on with a grace and determination that's amazing. But don't you think it's about time to forgive little Lisa? To stop denying her the good things in life because you decided so long ago that maybe she didn't deserve them?'

Lisa blinked as her tears evaporated. How

on earth could Hugh know those things about her when she'd only fleetingly given them any head space?

'You're allowed to want things just for yourself,' Hugh added. There was a twinkle in his eyes now. 'The things that make you feel good. Or to feel loved.' He picked up the bottle and began to pour a glass but when he held it out towards her, he paused, looking at her over the rim—like the way he had when she'd taken her first ever sip. 'Things like champagne,' he said. His fingers brushed hers as she accepted the glass and his words were a whisper that only she could hear. 'Or making love…'

Oh…*my*… Surely everybody in this café could see the glow that was about to reach Lisa's cheeks. But happiness like this was such a fragile thing, wasn't it? Irresistible but terrifying at the same time.

'I know.' Hugh was smiling at her. 'It's scary, isn't it? That was why I was such an idiot. I used my memories of the disaster that was almost my first marriage as a kind of shield to make sure I never took that kind of risk again. I took that shield out and polished it up when I realised I was getting in too deep with you. I was scared, too. I thought I'd get over missing you after you left but you know what?'

Lisa could feel her lips curling into a smile. 'What?'

'I just missed you more every single day. Until I finally realised that I had to trust my instincts. To trust *you*. As much as you were trusting me when you said you loved me. I'm sorry I got that so wrong... I wasn't ready, that's all...'

Lisa nodded. She could understand that. She could understand how hard it was to trust.

'I've never believed that the things I wanted just for myself were safe,' she told Hugh, her voice wobbling. 'They were just distractions and that made them dangerous.'

'I blame that doll,' Hugh said. 'With the stupid yellow hair.' His tone changed to something far more serious. 'You'll always be safe with me,' he said, 'if that's one of the things you want.' He drew in a deep breath.

'I love you, Lisa. Can you trust that? Can you trust *me*? Take that leap of faith?'

It was Lisa's turn to draw in a new breath. 'Could you hold my hand? So we could jump together?'

Hugh took both her hands in his. 'Always,' he murmured.

For the longest moment, they soaked in that connection. There would be time for the kind of intimate physical connection they knew would come later but the skin on skin of their entwined fingers was all they needed for this moment. The gaze on gaze of their eye contact was so deep it was a connection that felt like their souls were touching.

Nobody interrupted them but they were, after all, in the most romantic place on earth so perhaps a couple who were totally lost in each other's eyes was only to be expected. It had to stop eventually, of course, because a celebration was called for. Hugh filled the second flute with champagne. And then he reached into the inside pocket of his jacket and took out a third glass. He turned his head before he began to fill it, nodding towards the reception area of the café. Seconds later, Abby was rolling towards their table with the happiest smile Lisa had ever seen on her face.

'So you did it?' she asked Hugh. 'You proposed?'

'Oh, no...' Hugh handed Abby a glass of champagne. 'I forgot about that bit.'

Abby put her glass down. 'No champagne allowed then. Get on with it.'

Lisa laughed. '*Abby*—you can't say that.'

Abby scowled. 'But it was part of the plan.'

'It was,' Hugh agreed. 'And I had it all planned—apart from the ring because I'd want you to choose exactly what *you* want. But I just missed the perfect opportunity, didn't I?' He arched an eyebrow at Abby. 'A *private* opportunity.'

'It's not too late,' Abby said. 'Don't mind me. I want to read the menu again anyway.'

Lisa was still smiling. 'You don't have to do what she says.'

But Hugh had caught her gaze again and her smile faded. 'We never said a proper goodbye, did we? That last day of the cruise?'

'No…' It wasn't something Lisa really wanted to remember. It was a bit shocking, in fact, to have a reminder of how broken-hearted she'd felt, walking away from Hugh.

'There was a good reason for that, even if neither of us knew it at the time.' Hugh was still holding her gaze. He'd taken hold of her hand again as well. 'I never want to say a "proper" goodbye to you, Lisa Phillips. I want you to be in my life for every day I'm lucky enough to get. Will you marry me?'

Oh… Lisa was so ready to take that leap. Straight off the edge of that cliff, and she could do it without hesitation because Hugh was holding her hand. And she knew he would always be there to hold her hand.

'Yes,' she said softly.

'What was that?' Abby raised her head from the menu. 'I didn't quite hear it.'

'Yes,' Lisa said, more loudly. She was laughing again. So was Hugh. 'Yes, yes, *yes…*'

EPILOGUE

Two years later...

IT WAS NEVER going to get old, hearing the pop of a champagne cork. Not that they did it all that often but it always made Lisa smile. Perhaps that was because there was always that moment when she would catch her husband's gaze and know that they were both remembering that first time.

And celebrating their engagement, and later on their wedding, all in the same place, on the terrace of that magical café in the South of France. It was one of those private moments when so much could be said with nothing more than a fleeting, shared glance. It was fleeting, because they were here for something—and someone—other than themselves.

'Happy house-warming, Abby.'

'Thanks, Lise. I can't believe I'm here. That I actually have this incredibly cool apartment that's been custom built just to make life easier for me. And it's all thanks to you.' She raised her glass but then grinned. 'Oh… I almost forgot. You're not even going to have a taste, then?'

Lisa shook her head, her hand protectively smoothing the roundness of her belly. As if acknowledging the touch, her baby kicked against the palm of her hand.

Abby touched Hugh's glass with her own instead. 'It's thanks to you, too, bro. If you hadn't given me the heads-up that my dream job was coming up at your hospital, I wouldn't have thought about moving at all.'

'You're going to love it at St John's Hospital. I'm coming up to a year in the emergency department there and I'm still loving it.'

'Hey, it's a specialist hand therapist position in a team that's so good, people come from all over the country to get their surgery and start their recuperation. I still can't believe how lucky I was to get the job.'

'Why wouldn't you?' Lisa was beaming proudly. 'We're not the only ones who think you're the best. And it's Gran we should toast as well. If she hadn't made a good choice when she bought that little house decades ago, it wouldn't have sold for enough to make it possible to do a makeover like this on this apartment.' She looked around at the sleek lines and open spaces that made it so easy to live in for someone in a wheelchair but it still had the character that went with the old building it was part of, like the high ceilings and feature fireplaces.

'Best of all, you're a lot closer to us now,' Hugh put in. 'For, you know…those baby-sitting duties that are coming up.'

The ripple of laughter was comfortable. So was the teasing. They were a family unit now and about to welcome the first of the next generation.

'It's just a shame you're not having twins,' Abby said. 'Or triplets, even.'

'You're kidding, right?' Lisa shook her head. 'Why would you wish that on me?'

'You've got all those bedrooms in that

mansion of yours. You'll need to have a few more kids to fill them up. How are your parents doing, Hugh? Do they like their downsized life in Central London?'

'They're hardly ever there. It's ironic that when Lisa and I gave up working on the cruise ships, they decided that it was their favourite way to travel. They're on their way to Alaska as we speak.'

Hugh had come to stand behind Lisa and he put his arms around her, his hands over hers on her belly. The kick this time was stronger and Lisa glance slid sideways to find Hugh had done the same thing. It was another one of those private moments and it was so filled with joy that she couldn't look away.

'Oh, get a room,' Abby growled. 'No, wait…that's how this happened, wasn't it? I'll consider myself warned.'

It was a joke but Lisa could sense something in her sister's tone that made her move to give her a hug. A note of longing, perhaps? She knew Abby was thrilled with her new life that included her dream job and the perfect apartment but Lisa wanted for Abby the kind of happiness she had found with Hugh. Because it made life about as close to perfect as it could get.

'It'll be your turn one of these days,' she murmured as she wrapped her arms around her sister. 'You just wait and see…'

* * * * *

LET'S TALK
Romance

For exclusive extracts, competitions
and special offers, find us online:

facebook.com/millsandboon

@millsandboonuk

@millsandboon

Or get in touch on 0844 844 1351*

For all the latest titles coming soon,
visit millsandboon.co.uk/nextmonth

*Calls cost 7p per minute plus your phone company's price per
minute access charge

Want even more
ROMANCE?

Join our bookclub today!

'Mills & Boon books, the perfect way to escape for an hour or so.'

Miss W. Dyer

'Excellent service, promptly delivered and very good subscription choices.'

Miss A. Pearson

'You get fantastic special offers and the chance to get books before they hit the shops'

Mrs V. Hall

Visit millsandbook.co.uk/Bookclub and save on brand new books.

MILLS & BOON